SORCHA

CLOVER SPRINGS BRIDES 3

RACHEL WESSON

LONDONGATE PUBLISHING

❀ Created with Vellum

CHAPTER 1

BOSTON, WINTER 1882

Luke was dead.

Sorcha looked up from the letter, tears streaming down her face. Her hopes and dreams had died with him. She threw the pillow from her bed across the room. It just wasn't fair. She couldn't be stuck in Boston. That wasn't the life she wanted. *But it's what you deserve. Nobody loves you. Your Ma dumped you and ran. You are so ugly.*

Usually Sorcha could distract herself from the voice in her head but not today. She lay across the bed wallowing in self-pity. Laura came in sometime later.

"Sorcha, what's the matter? Did Mother Superior say something?"

Sorcha didn't look up but spoke with her head on her hands. "Luke's dead. My life is over."

"Your life? How do you think Luke's family and

friends feel? How about Mary? She knew him. He was only someone you had exchanged a couple of letters with." Laura clipped the back of Sorcha's head but in a gentle way.

It was enough to bring her to her senses. She sat up, shame causing her stomach to roil. Laura was right, as usual. Here she was wallowing in self-pity when Luke, dear kind lovely Luke, was dead.

"What happened?" Laura asked, looking at the letter. "Are Mary and her husband all right?"

Sorcha took a deep breath trying to stop the tears.

"Yes, they are fine. Seems Luke came across some young cattle rustlers. They were only starving kids but the gun they were holding went off. Luke died instantly."

"Well, at least he didn't suffer." Laura moved back to her bed, fixing her pillow before lying down.

Sorcha looked at the letter in her hands. *He didn't suffer. No, but I am. I was in love with him. He wrote me such lovely letters.* He had asked her to go to Clover Springs to become his bride. She had been counting the days until she turned 18. What was she going to do now? She let out a sob, closely followed by a series of others.

Getting up, Laura moved onto Sorcha's bed. She put her arm around Sorcha in an uncharacteristic display of affection. "Come on, let's go down and see if

Cook has any tea left. You Irish say that's the cure for everything."

"What am I going to do, Laura? I can't stay in Boston. I won't go work for Mr. Shepherd. I hate the way he looks at me."

Sorcha felt Laura shuddering. Her friend didn't like Mr. Shepherd either, but Mother Superior did. He came to the orphanage often, his gifts under one arm and his wallet in the other.

Just the day before, Mr. Shepherd had put his arm around Sorcha's shoulders. She could still smell his breath as he whispered into her ear. His boasts of the large donation he had made to secure her employment still rang in her ears.

It was amazing just how blind Mother Superior could be if there was a donation to the orphanage being offered. *May the Lord forgive me for such unchristian thoughts!*

"Come on, the kitchen's warmer than here. Cook might have some cake too. I'm starving."

Sorcha wiped the tears from her face and followed Laura to the kitchen. *Please God, help me get out of here before I am forced to take up employment with Mr. Shepherd.*

LATER THAT EVENING, Sorcha bit her pen as she composed the letter to Mary. How could she tell her friend she still wanted to come to Clover Springs? She didn't want to be a burden on anyone. Nor did she want to appear heartless, saying she was still intent on traveling despite Luke dying. But the alternative didn't bear thinking about.

"I am desperate, Mary. I cannot go to work for Mr. Shepherd. Please think of some way to get me to Clover Springs. I will do anything. I know you are just married but maybe there is someone in Clover Springs who wants a maid or even a wife. Anything is better than staying in Boston."

CHAPTER 2

CLOVER SPRINGS, COLORADO

"Sorry, Pa, Meggie was crying and I forgot about the dinner." Jenny sniffed.

Brian took a step towards his daughter but stopped as she cowered away. His child was terrified. Did she think he would hit her because she burnt some beans? She was only a child herself. *Abby should be here cooking and cleaning. God, why did you have to take my wife and boy? Haven't I paid enough for the sins of my father? Can't you see my children need their mother?*

Jenny did her best but at nine, she couldn't be expected to run a household. She couldn't keep herself clean, let alone a three-year-old who was prone to tantrums. It took a while to realize Jenny was still staring at him, waiting for him to say something. Meggie looked at him too, before going back to her game. She was banging some pans on the floor.

"I'm fed up of beans anyway. How about some eggs?"

Meggie stopped banging to grin up at him. "Yes, Pa." She lisped "Meggie like eggs."

He tickled Meggie under the chin and started over preparing their evening meal. He was bone tired having worked all day, and he still had chores to see to. But his children needed him first. The milking and such could wait till later.

Once the chores were done and the children asleep, he sat in the rocker facing the fire. Mrs. Sullivan was right. He needed a wife.

When Abby and Ethan were killed, Katie Sullivan was quick to offer help and support. She had watched over the girls for a few weeks, even showing Jenny how to prepare some simple suppers.

At first, he hadn't liked her coming to the house. He wasn't rude but he didn't make small talk. She had her job at the store, in addition to being newly married, yet she still found time to help his family. She ignored his attempts at coolness. She told the girls stories of life in Ireland and her family's trip across the water. He had listened in spite of himself. To be truthful, he missed those days when he had some adult company. The girls were lovely but they weren't up to making conversation.

Daniel Sullivan was a lucky man to have such a

brave wife. Mary, Davy's wife, was also a fine woman. Maybe he should write to Mrs. Gantley and see if she could find him a mother for the girls. He needed a housekeeper, and it would be nice to have someone to talk to. If he could get away without being married he would, but it wasn't proper for an unmarried woman to live out on the ranch with him.

What he needed was an older widow like Mrs. Higgins. *Maybe not that old.* Someone who didn't have dreams. A realist. He wasn't interested in replacing Abby. By taking away all he loved, God had shown Brian he wanted him to remain alone. He wasn't about to start a new family and put them at risk too. He had killed enough people.

CHAPTER 3

Katie picked up the letters, turning them back and forth in her hand.

"Reading other people's mail is a crime, you know."

Katie started, she hadn't heard Daniel come up behind her. "Oh, you startled me." Katie kissed his cheek before turning her attention back to the letter. "One's from Mrs. Gantley. I wonder if she's found Mr. Petersen a wife."

"Guess he'll tell you soon enough. He's due in town on Sunday. Said Angel would be all better by then. Why you had to call an old work horse Angel is still a mystery."

"Why couldn't she write me at the same time? She must know I would want to know. At least Mary is due in, so she can tell me what her letter says. I think it's from one of the orphanage girls."

Daniel laughed. “Katie Sullivan, you haven’t changed a bit. You were behind the door when God was dishing out the gift of patience.” Still laughing, Daniel wandered to the back of the store, leaving Katie at the counter still examining the letter.

Mary jumped down from the wagon. Davy had to check on some supplies, giving her time to socialize a little with Katie and Ella. She loved the baby, even though she appeared to have taken her temperament from her namesake. Mrs. Grey hadn’t mellowed much since Ella’s birth. She still gave everyone a piece of her mind. The only people she seemed to like were Ellen and baby Ella. Anyone seeing her with the baby would think she was the little girl’s doting grandmother.

“Have you the kettle on, Katie? My throat is parched.” Mary pushed the door of the store open as she talked. The bell tinkled.

“Ellen, will you mind the store? I want to go upstairs with Mary for a cup of tea.”

“Hello, Mary. Of course I will, Katie, so long as you take Ella.”

Katie thanked her sister before whispering to Mary. “Ella is so cranky today we couldn’t give her away.”

Mary took the baby and followed Katie up the stairs to the rooms above, trying to ignore the yearning she had. It had been months, yet there was no sign of her having a child. Maybe she was barren. She glanced over at Katie. Could she ask her? Davy had asked her not to say anything. He was convinced God would send them a child in his own time. That was all well and good, but he didn't seem to share the same need Mary had.

"Penny for your thoughts."

Katie's voice intruded on her thoughts. It wasn't the time to share her worries. Mary forced a smile on her face. "Your daughter is growing more beautiful by the day."

"She is when she's asleep." Katie took a sip of tea. "A letter came from Mrs. Gantley."

"How is she? How's Nellie? Does she ever visit the orphanage? I wonder how Ben is doing?"

"You're worse than me. The letter is addressed to Brian Petersen. I was tempted to steam it open. But for some reason, my husband didn't approve."

"You are a tonic, Katie. Whenever I am feeling sad, I know you will make me feel better."

Concern flitted across Katie's face. *Why didn't I bite my tongue?*

"What's wrong, Mary? It's not Davy, is it? I thought you were happy together."

"We are." Mary rushed to reassure Katie.

"So what is it?"

"I'm lonely. I know that sounds silly when I have

Davy and Mrs. H. But it's not enough. I miss the girls from the orphanage."

"Not just the girls."

"I never could keep anything from you. I'm worried about Ben. Sorcha said he wasn't happy. He keeps getting into trouble. I wish he wouldn't upset Mother Superior. She can be an awful old witch."

Mary stood to put Ella back in her cradle. She held the cup of tea between her hands savoring its warmth. She didn't want to look at Katie. The tears would start falling and it was getting harder to stop them.

"Sorcha will look after Ben, you know that. I know she will be leaving the orphanage soon but someone else will step in. He'll be fine. Come on, sit down and drink your tea and put a smile on your face." Katie took a gulp of her own tea. "I had a letter from Father Molloy. He was asking for you. He said he'd love to come out for a visit."

"Father Molloy come here? To Clover Springs. He's too old to make the trip."

"I wouldn't go telling him that. In his head, he is still twenty. He said he met some people from Galway on the latest ship to arrive from Ireland."

"Anyone we knew?"

"I didn't recognize the names but you might." Katie handed Mary the letter to read. Mary shook her head as she read through the list of names.

"It's shocking they murdered Lord Cavendish and Mr. Burke. If they catch those fellas, they'll hang." Katie pulled the cover back up on her daughter.

"I believe in Ireland belonging to the Irish but that doesn't make killing people right. What good will it do anyone?" Mary spoke as she continued to read. "That Parnell fella seems to have his head screwed on right, doesn't he? Father Molloy likes him too. He said he condemned the murders. Maybe he will win freedom for Ireland."

"He might, but I wouldn't bet any money on it. Father Molloy said feelings were running high amongst those who had lost families in the famine or to emigration."

"Would you go back, Katie?" Mary ignored Katie's look of surprise. "There are some days I would give anything to see home again."

"Home? Clover Springs is my home. Charlie Stanton's pigs would fly over the church bells before you get me back on one of those ships." Katie reached across the table to take Mary's hands. "Is there anything I can do, a chuisle?" Katie's Gaelic endearment made Mary smile. "I don't like seeing you so sad or hearing you talk this way."

Mary dipped her head. Taking a deep breath, she patted Katie's hand before standing up. "Don't mind me. I'm an eejit. Haven't I a lovely husband and a nice house? What more could a woman ask for?" *A baby*. Mary forced those thoughts out of her head. "Tell Father Molloy to behave. He's not to be upsetting Cook with his talk of Parnell and home rule."

Katie smiled, but her eyes were full of concern. Mary knew she wasn't fooling her friend. "Come on, I need to get the shopping done before Davy comes back. He'll not be happy if I delay him."

"Oh Mary, what's the matter with me! You got a letter too. I left it downstairs."

CHAPTER 4

Katie ran to get the letter leaving Mary alone with Ella. She picked up the child and hugged the baby close. *Please, God, give me a child. Soon*. She followed Katie downstairs to the store, swapping Ella for the letter. Ripping it open, she scanned the contents.

"It's from Sorcha. Oh, the poor girl. That Mother Superior, she's an awful…"

"Mary Sullivan. Least said, soonest mended, remember."

"Ach, I know but that woman! Sorcha wants to come to Clover Springs. She is adamant. She'll marry anyone. She doesn't want to have to go to work for Mr. Shepherd. Can't say I blame her either."

"ARE you sure that's what you want?" Daniel asked his brother as they packed their wagon.

"I want Mary to be happy. She lost so much already. She writes ten page letters to her sister Cathy to get a note back. Ben can give her the family she craves."

"What about when your own family comes along? You can't chuck the boy aside."

"Daniel Sullivan, what type of man do you take me for? If God gives us children, we will love them too. Ben needs a home. Mary wants a child." Davy threw the last sack in the back of the wagon. "Anyway, the old nun could say no. Mary said she was difficult."

"Well, from what the girls said about the orphanage, the nuns consider cripples to be a burden. I hope you know what you're doing. I mean, I admire you for giving a child a home but a cripple on a ranch?"

"It'll be fine." Davy spoke sharply. He wasn't sure who he was trying to convince more, his brother or himself. "Don't tell a soul. Do you hear me? Especially not Ma or your Katie. That pair couldn't keep a secret if their life depended on it."

"Katie will see the letter from the orphanage. You know she'll ask questions."

"She won't ask if the letters go to Father Cleary. Reverend Tim suggested I ask the priest to write to the nun in charge of the orphanage. He thinks the whole adoption will run smoother this way. You know what priests and nuns are like."

Daniel clapped Davy on the back. "Reverend Tim. He always has the answer. Who else knows about this?"

"Just Mrs. H but she is sworn to secrecy. Anyway, if you see Reverend Tim, ask him to call out to the ranch as soon as he hears anything. I won't be back in town until Sunday."

They both looked up as the store door opened and their wives appeared.

"I thought you had gotten lost." Davy took Mary's hand to help her up onto the wagon. "Did you solve the world's problems?"

"Away with you, Davy Sullivan. You were having a fine chat with my husband." Katie looked up at Mary with a twinkle in her eye. "How come when a man talks to a man, it's important business but with women, it's always gossip?"

The two men laughed.

"I am not answering that. I value my life too much." Daniel said as he wrapped his arm around Katie's waist. "Come here, Mrs. Sullivan, and give me a cuddle."

"Will you stop that, Daniel Sullivan? It's the middle of the day. What will…"

"Mrs. Grey think?" The rest of them chorused before Mary and Davy drove off laughing down the street.

CHAPTER 5

Brian stared at the letter. "She didn't have anyone suitable. How hard could it be to find a woman willing to come west?" He didn't realize he had spoken aloud until looking up he caught the look of sympathy on Katie's and Mary's faces. He lowered his eyes from their speculative gaze. He didn't like pity. He shoved the letter in his pocket and turned to leave.

"Mr. Petersen, please wait. We weren't sure what the letter would say. We would have been happy to welcome your bride but…" Mary fell silent as if regretting what she had said. "We asked you to step inside the store as I have a suggestion if you'd like to hear it."

He turned back to look at Mary Sullivan, her face

crimson. She wringed her hands in front of her skirt. He waited but she didn't say anything.

"Go on."

"My friend, Sorcha Matthews, wants to come live in Clover Springs. She is a lovely girl, very affectionate and loving. She is great with young children, having had a lot of experience in the orphanage. That's how I know her. We shared a room in the orphanage back in Boston. Katie doesn't know her." Mary stopped to take a breath.

"Wow, Mrs. Sullivan. Do you always talk so fast?"

Mary's face flushed and she stared at the floor.

"My apologies, Mrs. Sullivan. I was rude. Do you think that this Miss…"

"Matthews."

"…Miss Matthews would agree to becoming my wife?"

Mary's eyes lit up with pleasure. "Yes, I am sure she would. She was going to come here to marry Luke but he died. You know…" Mary stopped. "I'm doing it again. Sorry. Davy says I could chat for Ireland."

"Mary, don't you think Sorcha may be a little young?" Katie's question caused Brian to look at her. Her flushed face suggested she had concerns.

"How old is this girl?"

"Seventeen." Katie answered just as Mary said "Eighteen."

Mary stuttered. "She can't leave the orphanage till she is eighteen. But her birthday is next month."

"Maybe Mrs. Sullivan is right? Eighteen is rather young to take on two children. She might prefer to marry someone closer in age."

"Sorcha won't care. She is desperate to get away from Boston." Mary twisted her hands in her apron, looking everywhere but at him.

"Why?"

Mary's silence spoke volumes.

"You might as well tell me the truth." He spoke bluntly. He needed to know.

"Sorcha's mother, well she wasn't, that is..." The heat from Mary's blushes could start a fire. He tried to make it easier for her.

"She wasn't married?"

Mary shook her head. Brian knew he shouldn't be having this conversation with ladies, but the reality was his children needed a mother. There wasn't anyone else.

"If she lives in an orphanage, what difference does it matter what her mother did? Can she not just get a job in Boston?"

Mary exchanged a look with Katie before staring back at Brian. "The nuns have other ideas. They do not believe that a..., well I refuse to call Sorcha that name, will amount to much."

Brian's anger nearly consumed him. People were writing off this girl because of her mother's sin. *Just as they blamed me for Pa.* "If she's willing, I'll marry her. Just warn her, I come as a package. I need a housekeeper and mother to my children. I have no wish to, ahem, expand my family. If she is willing to agree to those terms, I will send her the train fare in time for her birthday."

"Do you not want to exchange a couple of letters with her before you make up your mind, Mr. Petersen?"

Brian looked straight at Katie in response to her question. "I don't have the luxury of time, Mrs. Sullivan. My children need a Ma. If Miss Matthews is agreeable, we will marry as soon as she arrives in Clover Springs."

Katie looked as if she wanted to say something but Mary interrupted. "Will you write to her inviting her to come? It would be better if it came from you. Sorcha is a lovely girl with a warm heart but she is a bit of a dreamer. She believes in happily ever after."

"That will soon change. Life doesn't offer any guarantees. We are all proof of that." Brian noted the look of shock on the ladies faces but he wasn't prepared to go along with any subterfuge. He was offering the girl a chance at a new life. Nothing more. Taking a pen from the counter, he scribbled a quick letter offering to marry the girl. He handed it to Mary.

She held it for a second before folding it over. "You can read it if you wish. I won't mind. Here's her train fare and a little extra should she need anything." Keen to get away, he tipped his hat at the ladies and walked out the door.

CHAPTER 6

BOSTON

"Laura, wake up. It's important."

"What's so important it can't wait until morning?" Laura grumbled.

"I've had another letter. Mary suggested I marry someone else."

Laura sat up. "Why didn't you say something earlier?"

"He's old." Sorcha stared at the letter wishing Mary had enclosed a description of the man she'd marry.

"Mr. Shepherd, old?" Laura's incredulous tone suggested Sorcha was mentally ill if she considered marrying someone of advanced years.

"No, not that old. But he's twenty-eight and has two children aged nine and three. Girls. They need a mother."

"You're only seventeen. You can't be a mother to a nine-year-old."

Sorcha shushed her friend. She always spoke loudly when something annoyed her. "Mary says he seems nice and the girls are lovely. It wouldn't be much different from looking after the young ones here. It's not like I don't have lots of practice with children."

"Sorcha Matthews, you can't be serious! What would your mam think if she was still alive?"

"My mam probably is alive. She wouldn't care." Sorcha regretted the words as soon as she spoke but she couldn't take them back now.

"How can your mam be alive and you live here? It's an orphanage, you know!" Laura said smartly.

"My mam didn't want me. She ran off to marry someone a year or so after I was born. Her mam, my granny brought me up. I didn't know she wasn't my mam until some kids told me. I thought they were lying when they called me a bas... well, that word." Sorcha fell silent for a few minutes, trying to block out the hurt those children had caused.

"I keep thinking of her. My real mam. She could be out there somewhere. Maybe she will come to Boston looking for me. I can't go to Clover Springs. She would never find me."

Laura sat up a little. "Darling, she's never going to

come for you now. You've lived here longer than most of us." Laura punched her pillow hard before lying back down. "Mary wouldn't tell you to pick a man unless he was a good one. She knows what it is like for us here. It's not like you have many options. Stay here and you will end up working for Mr. Shepherd. Leave and marry this man. Now go back to sleep."

Laura's right. She isn't coming back now. Maybe she's dead. Or she's married and had more children? I could have a real family out there somewhere. But they wouldn't be your family. Nobody wants the love child, do they? Why even call it a love child? There was no love involved where Sorcha was concerned. That's not true. *Granny loved me.* In her own way. Closing her eyes, she concentrated on remembering her granny's voice telling her bedtime stories of Irish myths and legends. But it was no use, she couldn't sleep.

Taking Mary's letter and the note from Mr. Petersen in her shaking hands, she read them through once more, her hopes rising with every word. God had heard her prayers. She was free. Clover Springs was her new home, and Brian Petersen was her knight in shining armor. She would be the best mother his children could ever have. She couldn't wait to meet the man who had saved her. She would see Mary again too. *Thank you Lord.*

CHAPTER 7

"So, you are leaving us? You didn't see fit to tell me you had been corresponding with Mary Ryan, planning this whole thing?"

Sorcha stared at the nun. Her face was so flushed beneath the wimple, she looked like her head may just blow off. Sorcha tried her best not to smile at the image as the nun ranted on. Then she stopped. Silence reigned. Sorcha didn't open her mouth. She couldn't be shouted at for something she didn't say.

"Are you simple? When someone asks you a question, they expect an answer."

"Sorry, Reverend Mother. I didn't realize you asked me anything. I thought you were lecturing me."

Sorcha heard Sister Una's intake of breath and saw Mother Superiors eyes narrow. She didn't care. She was eighteen and leaving. Nothing this woman could do mattered. Not anymore.

"You are brazen. Just like your mother. You can't hide from what's in the blood. May God forgive you."

Sorcha trembled but she wasn't about to let the nun tell lies. "God loves me, Reverend Mother. Granny always told me and she never lied."

The nun's eyes gleamed, causing Sorcha to shrink back a little despite herself.

"Your grandmother didn't know the meaning of the word truth. Didn't she try to pass you off as her own? She didn't tell you, your mother came back with your sister. Did she? She took one look at you and ran off faster than if the devil himself was after her."

"Reverend Mother."

Sorcha hadn't heard Father Molloy walk into the room, neither had the nun, given the look on her face. She had a sister. Where? What age was she? She stood, wanting to ask but her brain wouldn't engage.

"Come on child, let me get you a cab to take you to the train station." The priest smiled kindly at Sorcha, taking her arm gently. She was glad of the support. She was shaking so hard she didn't think she could walk on her own. *Mam had come back for her? With her sister?* Maybe she planned on them being a family. More likely she wanted to dump the sister on granny too. *She's lying.* But nuns didn't lie. Was she? Father Molloy's voice cut across the voice in her head.

"Mother Superior, we shall discuss this later."

The nun sat down with such a bump, her chair squeaked. Sorcha stared at her. She might have remained standing there but for the fact Father Molloy was pulling her after him.

"I am sorry your time here came to such a horrible end. I have no idea what came over the Reverend Mother."

"Father, she said Mam came back for me. I have a sister."

"Forget everything she said." The steel in the Father's voice brooked no argument.

"Yes, Father." Sorcha said automatically. *Did Mam really come back to find me? If she did, what happened to my sister?*

"Sorcha, you need to make the most of the opportunity God has seen fit to give you. Put the past behind you and look forward. Mary Ryan and Katie O'Callaghan are two of the finest girls you'll ever meet. They will look after you in Clover Springs. Sure you might see me there shortly."

"Yes, Father." Sorcha wasn't really listening as she spotted Laura waiting for her with one of the younger boys, Ben.

Laura hugged her close. "Write to me. Father

Molloy will bring them when he comes to see Cook. Don't forget me Sorcha, please."

"Laura, Mother Superior told me my mam came back with my sister. If she comes again, you'll tell her where I am, won't you?"

"Your mam? A sister? She's just playing nasty. She wants to upset you. Don't let her steal your happiness, Sorcha Matthews. She doesn't have power over you now. You're free."

Sorcha gave herself a quick pinch. Laura was right. She was free. She never had to step foot in this place again. She hugged Laura close, squeezing her hard. She whispered into her ear. "I won't. Be strong, Laura. Your chance will come too."

"It better, as Mr. Shepherd is going to be furious when he finds out you've left."

"He is not your future. Someone is looking out for us. Look what happened to Mary and now me. It will be your turn next."

Laura threw her eyes up to Heaven. "Still the dreamer, Sorcha Matthews," she whispered before giving her a quick hug and darting upstairs.

CHAPTER 8

Ben stood waiting at the door, his eyes glued to the floor. *The poor little mite looks terrified.*

"Ben, what are you doing here, and why have you a bag?"

The boy shrugged his shoulders, looking first at Sorcha, then toward Father Molloy, before looking back down at the floor.

"Ben is traveling with you, Sorcha. Please take good care of him before you hand him over to his new ma and pa." Father Molloy smiled, his eyes gleaming.

"I don't want a new ma and pa. I have parents. They will come back to get me." Ben stamped the floor, his angry gaze searing through the priest.

Sorcha hung back as the priest lowered himself almost to the ground.

"Ben, Mother Superior explained what happened to your parents."

"She didn't say anything other than they don't want me."

The priest sent an angry look toward the door of the nun's office. Sorcha was glad she wasn't in her shoes. She watched the priest as emotions fought on his face. Taking Ben's hand in his own, he said gently,

"Ben, your parents died a few months back during a fever epidemic. They are with God now."

Ben hiccupped but bravely held the tears in. "Where am I going? Why can't I stay here?"

"Well, you could, but don't you want to live with Mary Ryan?"

Sorcha thought her heart would burst right out of her chest at the look the boy gave the priest.

"Mary? She is going to be my new ma? Really?" Hope battled in the boy's eyes, but it was obvious he was having a hard time believing the priest.

"Yes, son, really, although she doesn't know it yet. Her husband, Davy, wrote to me and asked me to arrange a surprise for Mary. She has wanted you to come live with her ever since she left. In fact, she begged us to let you go with her. But with your parents being alive, we had to keep you here in case… well enough about that. Sorcha here is going to Clover

Springs and she will take you with her, if you promise to be a good boy."

"I promise, Sorcha. I'll be the best boy ever." Ben smiled through his tears.

Sorcha walked over to him and hugged him close. "I know you will." Not releasing her hold on the boy, she leaned toward the old priest and kissed him on the cheek. "Father Molloy, my granny would call you *Fear an chroí mhóir*."

The priest blushed scarlet. "Go away with you now, Sorcha Matthews. I try to be a man of God, not a man with a huge heart. He's the one with the big heart."

The priest hailed a cab to take Sorcha and Ben to the station. The pair waved at the small crowd standing outside the orphanage.

"Cook just gave Father Molloy her hanky, she's using her apron to wipe away her tears." Ben giggled. Sorcha smiled through her tears. She was excited at starting a new life but what if Mother Superior was telling the truth. What if she had a sister out there somewhere?

CHAPTER 9

CLOVER SPRINGS

Brian pulled at his collar. Was he doing the right thing? He saw the Sullivan's further along the station but he wasn't able to talk to anyone just now. His bride would be here any minute. An image of a brunette flashed into his mind. Abby had been his best friend at school. She had been there through all the hard times. They had married as soon as they were allowed. Abby loved being a mother. She often said, the only thing she wanted was to have a little home with healthy children and him.

Why did I insist on going to Church that Sunday? So you could pray for forgiveness. God had punished him. Why hadn't he died? Abby and Ethan were innocents. His skin crawled as the smiling face was replaced by one battered and bruised. They hadn't found his son. The river must have carried his body away. The sound of the train interrupted his thoughts. He brushed his hair out of his eyes. In a few minutes, his bride would be here.

"Will she be pretty, Pa?" Jenny asked.

He looked at his daughter, the image of Abby. His heart twisted again. Taking the squirming Meggie from her, he forced a smile. "It don't matter what she looks like. So long as she is kind to my girls."

"Do you have to marry her, Pa? I will work harder at home. I don't want a new Ma."

"We discussed this, Jenny. Don't question me again."

He ignored her scowl, chucked Meggie under the chin and stood straighter. Briefly, he wondered what his new bride would make of his family. Would she take one look at them and run?

CHAPTER 10

"Ben, stop squirming. We will be there soon. "

"I can't wait to see Mary. Can you believe she is going to be my new ma? I'm going to work really hard for her. She ain't never going to send me away."

Sorcha hugged the boy. "Isn't, not ain't. Of course she won't send you away. Mary loves you. She must have talked about you all the time if her husband sent for you. Clover Springs is a new start for both of us, Ben. No more sorrow. We are going to be happy every day."

"Sorcha, do you think he will mind…my leg?" Ben whispered, staring out the window.

"Ben, look at me now. Put any thoughts like that

out of your head. Mary and her husband will be lucky to have a son like you."

Ben didn't say anything but shifted closer to her. She put her arm around him. At least Granny had loved her. Ben, unfortunately, didn't know the meaning of the word until he met Mary. He'd lost her soon afterwards.

Sorcha squinted out the window trying to see her groom. He was her prince charming, her happy ever after. They would grow old together, surrounded by children and grandchildren. She would be respectable. *He said he didn't want more children.* She ignored the little voice in her head. *He couldn't mean it. Why look for a bride?*

She giggled at the sight of Mary wearing a blindfold. "Look Ben, do you see Mary waiting for us?"

The screech of the train brakes meant she didn't hear Ben's reply. She took his hand and moved to the door. Pushing it open, she let Ben get out first before following closely behind him. Her heart was beating so fast, she became dizzy. She held onto Ben tightly as if using him as a shield between her and the life that awaited her.

She spotted a tall man striding toward her. Was this Mr. Petersen? He held out his hand but she just stared at him for a couple of seconds.

"Miss Matthews?"

Sorcha nodded before swallowing hard. She struggled to speak but her words came out as a whisper. "Mr. Petersen?"

"No, sorry, Miss. I'm Davy Sullivan, Mary's husband. This must be Ben. Thank you for looking after him on the journey." Davy looked around him for a minute. Was he looking for Mr. Petersen? She stared around too, but didn't see anyone looking as nervous as she was. She tried to focus on what Mary's husband was saying.

"Why don't you both come with me? Mary can't wait to see you. She's over there with Katie, my sister in law. Petersen will find us, he may have gone to get your bags."

"I have everything I own right here, Mr. Sullivan. Perhaps he was delayed." Sorcha knew she wasn't succeeding in hiding her fear.

"No, he's here all right. I saw him not five minutes ago. Please come with us. Katie can't wait to hear how Nellie is."

At the mention of Nellie, Sorcha smiled brightly. She had only met Nellie a few times but she reminded her of her granny. "Nellie told Cook to tell me to watch out for Indians. She crossed herself when I said I couldn't wait to meet some."

Davy laughed loudly, causing a few people to stare in their direction. Sorcha relaxed slightly. If Mr.

Petersen was half as nice as Mary's husband, she would be very happy.

Davy bent down to be closer to the boy. "You must be Ben. I'm very pleased to meet you. Mary has told me lots about you." The boy stood taller. "She doesn't know you are coming, Ben. She thinks I've bought her some new books. I didn't tell her the nuns let you come to live with us. She is going to be so happy."

The child's face lit up with the biggest smile. Sorcha's eyes filled with tears. She gave Ben a quick hug before pushing him gently toward Davy.

"Come on, son. Let's go over to meet your new ma."

CHAPTER 11

Sorcha walked slightly ahead, wanting to see Mary's reaction to the surprise. For the moment, all thoughts of Mr. Petersen went out of her head.

"Miss Matthews, would you mind taking off Mary's blindfold, please?" Davy and Ben exchanged grins.

"Sorcha, I am so glad you are here. Sorry about my husband. He has an odd sense of humor. I don't know what you thought you were doing Davy..." Mary turned toward her husband but stopped talking to stare at Davy and Ben.

"Oh my. Ben, what are you doing here?"

Sorcha watched as Mary bent down to give the child a big hug. Tears ran down her friend's face. She wasn't the only one.

"Go on, son, give your new ma a hug." Davy said to Ben.

"Ma? You mean... Ben is ..."

Sorcha sighed loudly as Davy put his arm around Mary, kissing her on the cheek. "That's right. Ben is coming to live with us. Now stop fussing, woman, and take your son to the church. We need to find Petersen for Miss Matthews. We have a wedding to get to." Davy was nearly knocked off his feet as his wife gave him a huge hug.

Sorcha's stomach hit her boots. Mr. Petersen. She looked around her and spotted a man standing some distance away. He was fiddling with his collar, his attention on the two girls with him. He had to be waiting for her.

She moved toward him, leaving Mary chattering behind her. She wiped her hands down the side of her cloak, counting backwards in Irish as Granny had taught her. Granny said it was impossible to worry when you concentrated hard.

She faltered slightly as she walked down the platform. The man was huge, not only tall but also very broad. Her gaze dropped to his large hands, the tanned fingers covered in nasty looking scars. She flinched wondering how he had been hurt so badly.

He hadn't noticed her until she was almost standing beside him. "Mr. Petersen?" Her voice shook almost as much as the hand she held out. His eyes widened when he looked at her, but he didn't smile. He closed his eyes for a moment, not before she'd seen the pain and torment in their depths. Sorcha's heart beat faster. She had to make a big effort not to turn back and run to Mary. Her friend had her own family. This man and the girls were going to be hers.

The two girls were so different. The toddler was smiling at her but the older girl looked like she was going to spit. *Oh, I will have my work cut out there. Best start as I mean to go on.* She willed her feet to stand still as he took her outstretched hand. Mesmerized, she watched his giant palm take hers. She looked even smaller compared to him. They would be laughed at if they walked down the main street. She wished she was ten years older but then she wouldn't be in Clover Springs.

CHAPTER 12

She raised her eyes to his, surprised to find him also staring at their joined hands.

"I am Brian Petersen and this is my daughter Jenny –she's nine and Meggie is three." His voice was nice, quieter than she expected.

"Nice to meet you." Sorcha gave his hand a quick shake but he didn't let go. Electricity charged the air between them, causing the hair on the back of her neck to stand up. Flustered, she waited for him to break contact but several seconds passed. She risked looking up at him. He seemed to have had a similar reaction to hers, if the shocked look in his eyes was anything to go by. Dimly, she became aware of the children scrutinizing her. She pulled her hand loose before turning to the children.

She wanted to give Jenny a hug but the girl took a step back. Deciding she needed time to adjust, Sorcha turned her attention to Meggie squirming in her father's arms. "Aren't you a cute little thing?" The toddler beamed up at Sorcha, holding out her arms for a hug.

"Your children are beautiful, Mr. Petersen."

"Aye. They take after their ma."

Uncomfortable silence followed his remark. Sorcha trembled with jealousy? It couldn't be. She didn't even know his first wife. Not liking how she was feeling, she tried again with Jenny. "You are very pretty, Jenny. I like your dress."

"Don't lie. You know it's too small for me but Ma made it. My real ma."

Sorcha looked at her soon to be husband for some guidance on how to react but he stared at the ground. Jenny eyed her warily. She knew the child was hurting. It hadn't been that long since her ma had died.

"Yes, it is a little short but it is still very pretty. Your ma was an excellent seamstress. Do you enjoy sewing?"

Jenny appeared to have lost the ability to speak. Sorcha pretended she had answered positively.

"Great. Maybe you can teach me. I put the needle in my finger every time I try to sew something. My friend Mary, I mean, Mrs. Sullivan over there. She used to help me when we lived in Boston."

"Does your ma live in Boston?" Jenny asked.

Sorcha's stomach roiled. Why did a simple question about her parents upset her so much? "No Jenny, she doesn't. I haven't seen my ma for a very long time." Determinedly pushing all negative thoughts out of her mind, Sorcha stuck a smile on her face. It turned into a genuine one as she spotted Ben coming toward her. "Ah Ben, meet Jenny and Meggie Petersen. Girls, this is Ben. He's come to live with Mrs. Sullivan."

"Yeah, I got a new Ma just like you did." Ben smiled, happiness radiating from every pore.

Jenny stuck closer to her pa. "I don't need or want a new ma."

Sorcha bit the inside of her cheek.

"That's a horrible thing to say. Sorcha is the best. Well, not as good as my new ma, but just about. She is kind and she tells amazing stories about warriors and kings and magic."

Sorcha could have hugged Ben but it wasn't the right moment. She saw Jenny's interest was piqued, although the girl pretended otherwise. "Tsh, you boys are all the same. I don't want to know about wars or fighting or any of that stuff."

"Yeah, you girls are boring. She tells stories about princesses and queens and all too. In fact, she should tell you about the king's daughters. Their evil stepmother turned them into swans."

"That's enough, Ben." Sorcha said hastily as Jenny's face paled. Ben stuck his tongue out at Jenny before turning back to Sorcha. "Sorry, but she should be nice. She's getting a great ma."

CHAPTER 13

Tears threatened again as Sorcha hugged Ben. His loyalty was so unexpected, it almost pushed her over the edge. But she wasn't going to her wedding with tears flowing down her cheeks.

"Do you mind if I just talk to Mary for a couple of minutes? I didn't really get the chance as she was naturally excited about Ben coming." Sorcha asked, her voice shaking, but didn't wait for an answer. She hadn't promised to obey him yet. "Come on, Ben." She moved toward Mary, half dragging Ben behind her.

"Sorcha, darling. Thank you so much. I can't believe Ben is here. Finally." Mary wiped tears away.

"Don't look so scared. Being married is the best thing that ever happened to me." Sorcha let Mary take her arm, as her friend whispered, "Brian Petersen is a nice man and Jenny is such a character."

She's a character, all right. She hates me.

"And who could resist little Meggie? She makes me want to grab her and run. Isn't she just gorgeous?"

Sorcha couldn't help but smile. Mary hadn't changed. She still spoke a thousand words a minute. She heard the cough behind her at the same time Mary stopped talking. Her soon to be husband was standing, his discomfort obvious as he played with the hat in his hands.

"Excuse me, Mrs. Sullivan, but time is moving on. I don't want to keep Reverend Timmons waiting."

He looked everywhere but at her. This wasn't going at all according to her dreams. She looked to Mary, hoping her friend might rescue her, but her attention was once more fixed on Ben.

"Mary, are you coming to the wedding?"

"Isn't that a silly question? Of course I am coming. You don't think you would get married alone. I am sorry, Mr. Petersen, but Reverend Timmons can wait a few more minutes. A girl only gets married once and Sorcha needs to freshen up."

Sorcha bit back a giggle as her groom just stared.

"We will meet you at the church in, say, thirty minutes." Mary didn't give him a chance to agree but took Sorcha's arm and marched her down the platform. "Honestly, men haven't a clue about weddings, do they darling? Katie, you remember me talking about her, don't you? She's offered you the use of her home. The ranch being too far away. She went on ahead to heat up some water. You don't have time for a bath but you can clean up a little." Mary paused before adding. "I don't know how to thank you for bringing Ben out here. I can't believe my husband kept it a secret. I am such a lucky woman."

Sorcha walked, letting Mary chatter. She glanced behind her a couple of times. Mr. Petersen had stood staring after them for a few minutes before he had given in and followed them. She wondered if he was used to getting his own way. She watched how his children reacted to him. They didn't appear to be frightened or badly treated. Meggie was giggling and even Jenny looked brighter.

Please God, let this marriage work.

CHAPTER 14

They reached the store and went through to the back, where Katie had not only warmed up water but prepared a small snack as well.

"I remember the food on the train wasn't much. I bet you are rather nervous, but a little snack will help settle your stomach." Katie took Sorcha's black jacket. "It is so nice to finally meet you in person. Mary's told me a lot about you. I hope you will be as happy in Clover Springs as we are."

Sorcha sat. She couldn't speak. Her emotions were all over the place. The reality of meeting the man she would marry had fallen so far short of how she imagined it would be. Once a dreamer always a dreamer. She took a small bite of the sandwich but her stomach turned over. She pushed the plate away. "I'm sorry, but I think I am going to be sick."

"Oh, you poor love. You look scared to death. Mr. Petersen is a fine man. You will be grand." Katie took her hand and patted it while Mary poured a glass of water.

"Drink this. We know how you feel. Both of us were mail order brides too."

Sorcha didn't believe they understood. True they had married virtual strangers but they hadn't also inherited a family. *You're too young to be a mother to a nine-year-old.* Laura's words replayed over and over. She wanted the voice to stop. Standing too quickly, she let the dizziness take over and sank to the floor. She came round to find herself lying on the couch. "I'm so sorry."

"Don't move. Just relax for a few minutes. Sorcha, everything will work out for the best. Trust in God. He brought you here for a reason."

"I'm too young. Laura was right. Those children need a proper ma."

"Laura can go jump. I've seen you with the young ones in the orphanage. You are exactly what Jenny and Meggie need. Those girls lost more than their ma and brother, they lost their freedom. Mr. Petersen barely lets them out of his sight. They need you, Sorcha, just as much, if not more, than you need them."

Sorcha hoped Mary was right. She stood up slowly.

"Let's get to the church. I don't want to keep him waiting."

Katie returned to the room, carrying a small bunch of flowers and a pretty shawl. "I know it's not a wedding dress but it will go well with what you are wearing."

"It's beautiful. You can burn that hideous jacket. No more reminders of the orphanage. Put on the pretty shawl, Sorcha." Mary instructed, a fierce look in her eyes.

Sorcha handed the dark jacket over to Mary and placed the fine shawl around her shoulders. It was very soft.

"Davy asked if he could give you away." Mary smiled at her. "He wants to thank you for taking such good care of our son."

Sorcha wished she could swallow the frog in her throat. Everyone was so kind. She followed Katie and Mary downstairs. Ben grinned when he saw her. "You look good."

Davy burst out laughing, cuffing Ben gently. "Guess your new pa will have to teach you some lessons on how to speak to ladies, young man."

"I said she looked good. What's wrong with that?"

Everyone laughed.

"The expression you are looking for is beautiful. Every woman looks beautiful on her wedding day."

"Oh." Ben kicked at the ground, his ears and face crimson.

Mary put her arm across his shoulders. "Come on love, let's get going. Reverend Timmons won't wait forever."

CHAPTER 15

The group of them walked slowly across the town, reaching the church in a few minutes. The Petersen girls were sitting in the first pew, their father speaking to the Reverend. Davy held Sorcha's arm as the others took their seats. She walked slowly up the aisle to where Mr. Petersen waited.

The Reverend smiled but her face was frozen. She stared at the floor the whole way through the ceremony. She would have missed her vows if her groom hadn't gently squeezed her finger. Looking up at him, she was surprised to see pity and sadness in his eyes. She wanted him to swing her into his arms and declare undying love. Just like they did in the stories. She squeezed her eyes shut in a vain attempt to stop a tear escaping.

He had stared as she walked down the aisle, her

eyes fixed to the floor. Being tiny and delicate, she looked much younger than eighteen, not to mention fragile too. A cloak of desperation surrounded her. She would look more at home at a funeral given the expression on her face. Was it too late to stop the ceremony?

He could feel her shivering as she stood beside him. Why had he agreed to marry the girl? *Because you need a wife. Why marry a child then?*

Closing his eyes, he forced the negative thoughts away. His mind flew back to his first wedding. Abby had been shaking too, but she was excited not scared. They had grown up together and married as soon as their parents agreed they could. The church had been packed with her friends and family. Everyone loved Abby. Why was she taken? Why not him instead? He deserved to die. She didn't.

What if something were to happen to the girl standing beside him? That thought sent a shudder through him. He'd been wrong to put another innocent at risk. Desperately, he glanced around. He had to stop the service. Now.

He risked a glance at her. Big mistake, she was staring back up at him. Her eyes widened a little. She was still terrified but she also looked... hopeful, maybe a little trusting. Oh dear God, she must think this was the start of a good life. Maybe it was better than she was used to. Life in an orphanage couldn't be fun. What was it the Sullivan wives had said? Something about the nuns holding her background against her.

Dimly, he realized Reverend Timmons was clearing his throat. He looked at him, wondering why he was staring at him.

"I pronounce you man and wife. Again." Reverend Timmons whispered.

He'd missed the ceremony. Embarrassed, he turned to his wife and kissed her lightly on the lips. The contact sent shudders through him, the heat sending waves of warmth through his body. Surprised at his reaction, he noted a similar response in her eyes. The chemistry between them sent sparks flying. He was torn between wanting to push her away and pulling her into his arms to deepen the kiss. He forced himself to do neither. His life was complicated enough without falling for the child at his side. *Child? Who are you kidding?* She may be young but she was all woman. He hadn't been blind to the lovely figure hidden behind her pretty shawl but awful dress.

Pushing all thoughts aside, he thanked the Reverend. Picking up Meggie, he turned to Sorcha and suggested they head home. His tone was gruff causing her eyes to widen. He wasn't angry with her but with himself. He had no right to be thinking of her the way he had.

"Now?"

"I have chores to do and the children are hungry." He tried hard to mellow his tone. "I will bring you back to town on Sunday if you want to visit with your friends a little."

Sorcha didn't answer. She removed her shawl and handed it to Katie Sullivan, giving her a quick hug. She also hugged Mary and Ben. After nodding to the Sullivan's, Brian reached for Jenny's hand as he walked out of the church with his new wife trailing behind him.

CHAPTER 16

By the time he settled Meggie in the wagon, Sorcha was on the seat waiting for him. She stared straight ahead, her back ramrod straight. They rode home in silence. He glanced at her a couple of times but she said nothing. Just sat there chewing nervously on her lip. He should say something to ease her mind but what? What could he say to make this stranger feel better?

"This here is the start of my…our land, the house is over that rise. The cottonwoods are blocking our view but you will see it shortly."

He saw her squinting into the distance. She was a brave woman coming all this way to live among strangers. He resolved to make sure she never regretted coming to Clover Springs. *Keep your distance and she will be safe.*

"What is the big red building? Have you two houses?"

Her question interrupted his thoughts.

"That's the barn where I do most of my work. I built it a little ways back from the house. That way if I have to work through the night, I don't disturb Abby... I mean the girls"

Why did he have to mention Abby? Sorcha didn't seem to notice as she continued to stare at the barn. "There is a small yard outside where the horses can exercise as they get better."

"What do you work at? Are you a horse rancher?"

Brian tried not to roll his eyes. How wealthy did she think he was? She was in for a shock. "I'm a farrier." At her rather blank expression, he explained. "I look after horse's hooves."

"Ah, so that's what happened to your hands." She giggled as he stared first at his hands and then back at her. "Sorry, I laugh when I'm nervous. I noticed the scars and my imagination ran away with me. The nuns were always telling me I was too much of a dreamer."

He liked listening to her talk, her accent was very soft.

"We call people like you blacksmiths."

He smiled at her. "I guess you could have called me a blacksmith when I first started out. But my work now has little to do with making the shoes or fixing tools. I do sometimes but generally I let Frank do that work."

"So if Frank makes the shoes, what do you do?"

"You can't just shove a shoe on a horse. Or at least a decent horse owner wouldn't do that. You have to make sure it fits properly. Horses are like humans. Their hooves are all different sizes and they can develop bumps and lumps just like us."

"Pa speaks to horses. He thinks they can speak back." Jenny said. Brian glanced behind him to see her eyes rolling upwards.

"Horses don't speak, but they do communicate, Jenny. They can tell you when they are happy, sad or sick. You just need to listen to them."

"It sounds like you love your animals." Sorcha said as her cheeks pinked.

She was shy and he had almost dragged her out of her wedding. What sort of idiot would she think he was?

"You can trust a horse. Treat it right and it won't turn on you. Bit like dogs. No such thing as a bad dog, just poor owners."

"They didn't have any pets at the orphanage." Sorcha shrugged but he'd noticed her mouth grew tight anytime she mentioned the orphanage. She must have been desperate to leave if she came all this way to marry a stranger with two young ones.

"There were always cats but the children were discouraged from feeding them. A fat cat didn't make a good rat catcher."

"I would like to have a horse ranch someday." Brian surprised himself by admitting his dream. "But for now, I just fix them up and send them back. I haven't been working as often as I should what with the girls and everything."

"I can look after the girls now."

"Thanks." Brian pulled up outside a small house. "I will take the wagon back to the barn. See you for dinner."

"You mean you are not coming inside with us?"

"No, Jenny can show you where everything is. Make yourself at home. If you do go for a walk, stay away from the long grass."

"Why?" Sorcha looked at the acres of long grass, a curious look on her face. He'd expected her to be frightened.

"Snakes, that's why." Jenny said jumping out of the wagon, her tone suggesting Sorcha was stupid.

Sorcha grabbed her skirt closer. "Snakes? Are they dangerous?"

Brian laughed but quickly turned it into a cough at the look in her eyes. "Sorry, but you don't have to be scared of snakes in the wagon. They hide in the grass. Snakes don't like us any more than we like them. Most aren't too dangerous although they can give you a nasty bite."

"You'll hear the rattlers."

"That's enough Jenny." Brian focused on Sorcha who now looked terrified. "You just need to be sensible. Don't go walking in the long grass. Don't put your hand anywhere without looking first. If you do hear a rattle, step away slowly."

Sorcha gulped, balling her fists by her side. "Sorcha, please don't fret. We've lived here a long time and never been bothered by snakes. That's not about to change."

She didn't say anything and was still pale, but she sat up straighter in the wagon. He jumped down and walked around to her side. She lifted her skirts as he helped her, marveling as his hands almost enclosed her tiny waist. She was way too skinny to be healthy. Last thing he needed was a sick wife. Jenny helped Meggie down. His neck heated as he realized he was still holding Sorcha. He coughed and moved away quickly. "Jenny, help your Ma. I will be back later." He climbed back up onto the wagon and clicked the reins.

CHAPTER 17

Sorcha stood staring at his retreating back. He wasn't serious, was he? Was he playing some sort of joke? She hoped so and waited a couple more seconds. But the wagon disappeared around the back of the barn. She touched a finger to her lips remembering the sensations his kiss had evoked. She'd never been kissed before. Would he kiss her again later?

She twisted her fingers in the silver cross necklace. It made her feel safe. Granny said nothing bad would happen if she wore it close. But she'd been wearing it the day Granny died. Sorcha screwed her eyes shut to sever that line of thought. That road only led to pain.

Jenny and Meggie ran around the yard chasing some squawking chickens. The noise intruded on her daydreaming. Opening her eyes, she stared around her. She searched the ground looking for snakes but didn't see anything. *He said they hide in the long grass, stupid*!

In her dreams, she assumed she would live on a ranch like the one Mary described in her letters. She hadn't imagined living somewhere so small and so far from the nearest house. *It's better than the orphanage, isn't it?*

"Meggie's hungry. That's why she's crying." The sharp tone and the look the child sent her didn't hide her feelings. She hated her.

"Jenny, I will need you to help me. Everything is so new. You are a big girl and I bet you can show me how to make things just the way your pa likes."

Slightly disconcerted by the sudden smile on the young girls face, she dismissed it. An accommodating child was better than the sulky one who had accompanied them home.

Pushing open the door, they went inside the house. Her feet stuck to the kitchen floor. Looking around her, she surveyed the mess. The sink was full of dirty breakfast dishes, the fat congealing on top of the cold water. At first glance the table seemed clean enough, although the colorful cloth would benefit from a good wash. The benches on either side of the table needed a good scrubbing. Everywhere else was covered in a layer of grime. It looked like nobody had cleaned for weeks.

"I take it your pa isn't big on housework?"

"Cleaning the house is my job not Pa's. But you wouldn't know that, would you? You never lived in a house before."

Sorcha gripped the edge of the table. The child was asking for a slap. "Of course I lived in a house. Only it was much bigger than this and had lots more people." Jenny opened her mouth but before she could say anything, Sorcha intercepted her. "Right, let's get a hurry on. I will make something quick to eat but first can you show me around so I can find everything please."

Jenny grudgingly gave her a guided tour leaving her pa's bedroom until last. "This is Pa's room. I suppose you best leave your things in there."

The main bedroom had a pretty quilt covering a feather mattress. The window was dressed with matching curtains. Brian's first wife must have been good at sewing. She didn't want to dwell on the woman she had replaced. She put her satchel on the floor beside the closed trunk at the foot of the bed, grabbed an apron from a hook on the wall and returned to the kitchen.

Meggie's cries were becoming louder. Sorcha picked up two relatively clean cups and filled them with milk. There was some rather hard bread on the counter top. It looked ok. She cut it and spread some jam on top before handing it out to the girls. She would find the butter later. For now, it was more important to stop Meggie's crying. She didn't want Brian to come back and think she couldn't cope.

"Any suggestions on what I cook for dinner?" Sorcha had a quick look through the kitchen cupboards but there was little to choose from. Her new husband wasn't the best homemaker.

"Pa loves roast chicken. I haven't been able to make it for him but you could, couldn't you?"

"Sure, love, but a full chicken on a week day?"

"Pa was going to kill it ready for roasting but we were running late and didn't want to miss the train. Come on, I'll show you."

Picking up Meggie, Sorcha followed Jenny outside to the chicken coop.

"Ever killed a hen?" The look on Jenny's face made it easy to see she believed Sorcha to be useless.

You little madam, you are not going to get the best of me. Handing Meggie to Jenny, Sorcha picked up a large axe dragging it behind her. It was heavy. *Please let me kill it quick.* Amazing herself as much as the other girl, she caught and quickly killed the hen Jenny had chosen. She was delighted by the look of surprise on the children's faces. "Where I came from, there's not much time for sitting around looking pretty."

Jenny looked her up and down. "Good job, really."

Sorcha took a deep breath staring after the girl who was walking back toward the house. She couldn't have meant it the way it came across. She was only nine.

CHAPTER 18

Pushing aside her growing doubts about whether she would ever love her new stepdaughter, Sorcha held the chicken tighter. She quickly pulled out some feathers and took it back into the kitchen. It couldn't be that hard to roast it. She had seen Cook put chickens in the oven on a Sunday.

She knew how to set and light the fire in the stove, making sure the oven was hot before placing the chicken inside. Then she cleared up the dishes, prepared some vegetables and potatoes. She beat up a batch of biscuits. They would help the food stretch to provide enough for tomorrow's lunch.

Sorcha sang as she worked. Maybe it wouldn't be so bad after all. Jenny helped her around the house. She seemed rather clumsy but hopefully that was just a phase. But after one too many spills, Sorcha told her to take Meggie out to play. It was easier to do the chores herself rather than have to do them over again.

After a while, the girls came in saying they were hungry and cold. "What's that horrible smell?" Jenny wrinkled her nose as she looked toward the stove.

"I don't know. There might have been something on the floor of the stove. I didn't have time to clean it out properly." Sorcha knew by the look on Jenny's face she wasn't convinced. It couldn't be anything else. Roast chicken didn't smell like that.

She gave them a couple of warm biscuits and told them to go play outside. She kept the door open to help dispel the smell. Jenny was right, it was awful.

She moved to the door to get away from the stench. Watching the girls playing together gave Sorcha hope. Jenny played so nicely with her little sister. If she tread carefully, maybe she could win the young girl over.

Despite the smell in the kitchen, Sorcha was relatively pleased. The little house was cleaner than it had been. It wasn't perfect. The windows needed cleaning and there were no curtains in the main rooms. She would have to talk to Mary. She didn't know how to make new curtains.

She had changed the sheets on the main bed – the ones on it would have walked off by themselves had she left them there any longer. The girls shared a room off the kitchen. The sheets on their beds seemed clean. Sorcha decided they could wait another day or two. There was only so much she could do before Brian came home. She didn't have time for laundry today but would do it tomorrow. She hated washing clothes, her skin reacted so badly to the soap.

Laura used to tease her saying she must have been a real Lady in a prior life. Tears threatened thinking of the friend back in Boston. She had promised to write as soon as she was married. Smiling ruefully, she remembered the romantic wedding she'd told Laura she would miss. She'd never dreamed her wedding day would consist of a hurried ten minute service with no music or flowers, followed by a wagon trip to a small house miles from anywhere. *Think of Mr. Shepherd. Count your blessings.*

CHAPTER 19

Her hands sweated as the time raced by. All too soon, she heard the girls calling his name. Glancing in the mirror, she caught her reflection. Her flushed cheeks and unkempt hair didn't encourage confidence. She looked a sight and didn't feel much better. The smell from the oven was making her eyes water. There wasn't time to do anything though, as the door opened and he walked in.

"Evening. I hope the girls behaved." He took a step back. "What is that awful smell?"

Sorcha ignored the comment about the smell, thinking it best to give him good news. "Yes, they did. Jenny helped me with the chores before looking after Meggie. Are you hungry?"

"I was starving but…well, I don't mean to be rude but what exactly are you cooking?"

"Roast chicken. I think there may have been something stuck to the oven. Cook's never smelt like this."

"On a week night?"

Sorcha stammered. "I thought it was your favorite meal?"

"I tried to tell her, Pa, but she wouldn't listen. It was our best egg layer too." Jenny's tone was pitying.

Sorcha took a step back at the angry look on her husband's face. *What had she done?* "I'm so sorry. I just wanted to make a good impression. It's our wedding day, after all. I haven't ever had my own house. I ..." Sorcha stopped as he continued to stare at her, a funny look in his eyes.

"Sorcha, did you clean the chicken?"

"Of course, I cleaned it. I took the feathers off and...." She stopped as he started to laugh or was it cry. There were tears rolling down his face.

"I don't see what is so funny."

He didn't answer her but went to the stove, opened it and pulled the foul smelling roast out. He opened the back door.

"Open the windows and the front door. Girls, go outside now. Sorcha, bring whatever food you have and a blanket. We will eat under the big tree." Everyone stared at him. "Move unless you want to sleep with this stink."

The girls scrambled to obey him as he walked off with the roasting pan.

"Pa is real angry. I wouldn't want to be in your shoes later." Jenny said, grinning widely.

"That's a horrible thing to say."

"Maybe, but it's true." The girl ran off leaving Sorcha standing there with tears running down her face. She still wasn't sure what she had done wrong. But it was all a big mess. She plated up the rest of the meal and carried it out to the tree. Jenny had set a blanket on the ground. "Picnic." Meggie lisped beaming.

Sorcha watched Brian walking back. Her heart beat faster as she clenched and unclenched her fingers. Would he send her back? *You are married now. But he could divorce you.*

"Mr. Petersen." At the look he gave her, she stuttered. "Brian, I'm sorry. I don't understand what went wrong. Cook made it look so easy."

"Thank you for the effort, Sorcha. Jenny, take Meggie over to the pump and wash your hands. I want a word with your Ma."

"She's not my Ma."

Before anyone could react, Jenny was gone, leaving Meggie behind her. Sorcha moved to follow

"Leave her."

"But she's upset."

"She's my daughter. I said, leave her. Sit and eat."

Sorcha sat but didn't make any attempt to start eating.

"I appreciate it's your first day here and we have to get to know one another. I assume you didn't decide which hen to kill?"

Sorcha shook her head.

"I thought so. Jenny will come round in time. You're the adult and you have to set the example. Surely you know people like us don't sit down to roast dinners during the week?"

"Sorry." Sorcha repeated the apology. She felt like a chastised child.

"You'll learn. I appreciate you lived in the city. You obviously have never killed a chicken before."

Sorcha shook her head.

"You don't just chop off its head and pull out a few feathers. You have to clean it first and remove the innards. We couldn't have eaten the meat – it would have made us all ill."

Sorcha gasped, the tears threatening to fall. She was useless.

CHAPTER 20

The look on her face reminded him of Jenny when she got upset. Jenny. He fumed again. She had set Sorcha up. His daughter may be only nine but she had been raised on a farm. Brian tried to soften his tone.

"Eat. No point in letting more good food go to waste. It wasn't your fault. Jenny should have known better."

"Jenny knows how to kill a chicken properly?"

"She's never done it herself but she saw her Ma do it often enough. Please eat. You must be hungry. I will deal with Jenny later."

"What are you going to do?"

"That's none of your concern."

Sorcha dipped her head, clenching and unclenching her fingers. Her lips were moving silently.

"Mr. Petersen, sorry, Brian. We are now a family and if you want me to look after your children, they must respect me. Please let me discipline Jenny this time."

He stayed silent, staring at her for a couple of seconds. She was right, he had to let her manage the girls.

"Ok."

He picked up the knife and starting buttering some biscuits. "These are good." The look of surprise in her eyes hit him in the stomach. Had nobody ever complimented her before? "Sorcha, please eat. There is nothing to be gained from you making yourself ill. This… well, this situation was bound to cause some problems. We will learn how to get along. But not on an empty stomach." He handed her a biscuit.

Meggie giggled as she played with her food but the adults ate in silence.

"You are a good cook. I look forward to tasting your roast chicken but I will show you what to do first." He smiled, hoping she would smile back. Her silence was getting to him. She looked as if she was going to burst into tears. "Thank you." He stood up. "I have to get back to work. I will find Jenny and send her back to help you."

"Thank you. Would you like some coffee later?"

"No, thank you. See you tomorrow."

With that he was gone. Only then did Sorcha let

the tears fall. Picking up Meggie, she cradled the child to her.

Dear Lord what have I done? He doesn't want a wife and Jenny is plotting against me.

Meggie cuddled her head into Sorcha's neck, her chubby arms holding her tight. She sighed as she looked up at Sorcha before closing her eyes with a smile. "You are a beauty, little Meggie. Please don't change when you get older."

Carrying the young girl into the house, she shivered. It was nearly colder inside than out but at least the worst of the smell had gone. She settled the little one on the floor before going back for the blanket and the rest of the food. Carrying the dishes into the kitchen, she was glad she had stood her ground. She had to find a way to get Jenny on her side. But first she had to calm down. It wouldn't do anyone any good if she tackled the child tonight.

She continued working as she heard the door click softly behind her. She sensed it was Jenny. "Your dinner is on the hot plate. Sit down." Jenny didn't reply but took a seat. Sorcha put a plate of food in front of her.

"When you are finished, you can go to bed. We will talk tomorrow."

"But..."

"Tomorrow, Jenny. It's been a long day and I'm tired."

Sorcha finished her work in silence. She pretended to ignore the little girl as she ate and put her plate in the sink. The child went to her bed without saying goodnight. Sorcha sank into the chair beside the fire, putting her head in her hands. *Help me, please.*

She sat staring into the flames for a long time. All her energy was gone and she was too tired to get up. She waited to see if he changed his mind and came back.

Nodding off, she relaxed back into the chair. She must have been asleep for some time as when she opened her eyes, the fire had almost gone out. Sighing, she rose and went to the bedroom.

She lay in bed, her heart beating faster at every sound but he never came back. This wasn't what she had imagined at all. A tear escaped and ran down her cheek. Laura was right. She had dreamed too big. He wasn't interested in her. Any woman who could cook, clean and look after children would have done. She had dreamed so long of having a real family. Here she was, a husband and two children and she'd never felt lonelier in her life.

CHAPTER 21

Brian worked off his anger. The day had been a disaster. He'd made a big mistake taking on a young girl as a wife. A city one at that. Any fool knew you had to clean out an animal before you cooked it, didn't they? That wasn't fair. Living in the orphanage wouldn't have given her much opportunity to learn about stuff like that. But she had potential. The biscuits and vegetables she had cooked tasted great. Being young, she would learn quickly.

If only he had time to teach her. Jenny could. As soon as that thought came into his head, he dismissed it. He loved his daughter but she was as stubborn as he was. She had made it quite clear she wasn't happy having a new Ma. He'd never thought she would be cruel though. Abby would be distraught. She wanted her girls to be kind and gentle. There was nothing kind in tricking a woman in the hope of getting her sent away.

The horse neighed. "Sorry Jackson, was I too rough? I've a lot on my mind." He looked into the horse's eyes. "What am I going to do? I thought I was giving her a chance at a new life but maybe I was wrong. Meggie likes her but Jenny... she's a tough nut to crack." The horse didn't respond, but simply stared.

BRIAN THREW his bed roll to one side as the cock crowing woke him up. He must have finally gone to sleep, despite tossing and turning for most of the night. He'd gone soft sleeping in a bed for so long. His whole body ached from the hard floor.

He headed for the house, hoping the coffee was strong. Pushing the door, he was surprised to find the girls were still asleep. The stove had almost gone out and the pot was empty.

This is what you get for expecting her to take on a household. What experience does the average eighteen-year-old have, never mind one brought up in an orphanage? He threw some kindling on the fire, stoking it to encourage the flames. He banged a couple of pots hoping the noise would wake his new wife.

"Pa, what are you doing? I can cook breakfast." Jenny rubbed the sleep from her eyes.

"Go wake your ma."

Jenny stood, a scowl on her face. "Ma's dead."

He glared at her but before he could speak, Sorcha appeared. She didn't seem to realize her nightgown was transparent as she stood in front of the window. He looked away, the sight of her body was stirring his senses.

"I'm so sorry. I never sleep late. I don't know what happened. Please let me." She reached out for the pan promptly burning herself. She swayed as the pan dropped out of her hand. Grabbing her, he pulled her over to the sink and pumped cold water on the ugly red weal. "Take some slow deep breaths."

He could feel her shaking and saw the tears welling in her eyes. She looked terrified. Did she think he was going to beat her?

"It's the air. People say they sleep better out here than in the city." He was talking fast but it was best to distract her. "You had a long journey. Jenny should have had breakfast on the table. She managed up to now. Jenny, go get the switch." After her antics the night before and now this morning, Brian knew his daughter needed teaching a lesson.

"No, please don't. I can't bear seeing a child whipped." Sorcha touched his arm. "I am sure Jenny believed it would be better letting me do the cooking today. Isn't that right, Jenny?"

Jenny just stared, a bewildered look on her face.

"Go and get dressed." Brian tried to control his tone. If he wanted her to stay, he had to be civil. "I will cook breakfast this morning. Tomorrow you can take over."

Cradling her hand, Sorcha nodded slightly before walking quickly to the bedroom. When the door clicked shut, Brian turned to Jenny. "Young lady, don't push me too far."

CHAPTER 22

It didn't take long to cook some eggs and bacon. They sat together at the table, the adults having coffee and the girls drinking milk. Silence reined until the food was eaten.

"Does Jenny walk to school on her own?" Sorcha asked, standing to move the dishes to the kitchen.

"Jenny, go do the dishes for your ma." A glare from Brian was enough to stop any retort from the child. Sorcha took a step back as the girl brushed past her. Brian's next words took her full attention.

"She doesn't go to school. I teach her what she needs to know right here."

"School's important, not only for learning. How will she make friends if she never sees anyone but Meggie?"

"She don't need friends. The less people she has to deal with the better. That way she won't be hurt."

Sorcha knew Jenny was listening to every word of their conversation as she washed the dishes. She couldn't blame her. Tempted as she was to postpone the conversation until the girls were outside, curiosity won.

"Who'd want to hurt Jenny? She's only a young girl."

She saw him glance at Jenny before turning the full force of his gaze in her direction. He smiled but his eyes were hard.

"Sorcha, you mean well but these are my children and my house. I don't want the girls going to school and that's my final word. I have chores to do."

Speechless, she stared at the door. What was he hiding from? She slumped into the rocking chair. How was she going to deal with this? Surely he didn't mean to keep them all away from town. She wanted, make that needed, to see her friends.

CHAPTER 23

Sorcha sat lost in thought until she heard something behind her. Turning toward the kitchen, she spotted Jenny peeking out from behind the door.

"Come sit down here please, Jenny." Sorcha's tone left no room for argument

The girl stood in front of her.

Sorcha moved slowly on the rocker. She reached for Jenny's hand but the child moved away. "Listen sweetheart, I think we need to clear the air. You behaved very badly yesterday."

"Are you going to cane me?"

"No." Sorcha didn't hide the tremor in her voice. "I won't ever hit a child." At Jenny's incredulous look, Sorcha continued. "Jenny, where I lived, children like you and Meggie were hit every day."

"Meggie's only a baby. Nobody should hit her."

"Nobody will hit Meggie. But some children aren't as lucky as you and Meggie. They don't have anyone to look out for them so they have to go live with strangers. Sometimes those strangers don't treat them nice."

"But Pa said you lived with nuns. They are supposed to be kind."

"Yes, some of them are. Sister Una, she was my favorite, she used to cuddle the younger children. I never saw her hit anyone."

"So why did you leave then and come here? We don't want you. Pa doesn't either." Jenny pouted but her eyes filled with tears. Sorcha took a deep breath before speaking. She didn't want to start crying too.

"I think you should know a few things. I am not here to take your ma's place. I know nobody could do that." Sorcha waited for Jenny to say something but she didn't. Spotting a tear running down the child's cheek, Sorcha put her hand out again. This time, the child took it. Drawing her closer, Sorcha said quietly. "I would like us to be friends. Your pa would like that I'm sure." She wasn't sure of anything but that didn't matter now. The child's unhappiness and loneliness hung around her like a wrap. "I will have to help look after you just like you look after Meggie. You can treat me like a big sister if you want to. "

Jenny nodded quickly.

"After yesterday, you can see that I will need a lot of help looking after your pa. He told me your ma showed you how to prepare food. Would you teach me?"

Jenny bit her lip as if considering the request.

"I can bake. Cook showed me how to make pies and bread. I thought I could cook too but maybe I could do with more help. I don't think any of us wants to smell that stink again"

Jenny giggled.

"Why don't we do some baking now? Does your pa like pie?" Sorcha asked.

"Oh yes, pumpkin is his favorite."

Sorcha studied Jenny's face but didn't say anything. A couple of seconds passed as Jenny's eyes looked everywhere but back at Sorcha. "Oh, all right. He hates pumpkin but he likes apple."

"Are you sure?"

Jenny smiled. "I promise. He loves apple pie. I like it too. We go picking apples and cherries. Or at least we did when Ma was alive."

Tempted as she was to envelop the girl in a hug to help her through her grieving, instinct made her move slowly. She had to earn Jenny's trust first.

"Okay then. Let's go make him a pie."

Sorcha included both girls in the pie making. In no

time at all they were covered in flour but at least they were smiling. Leaving them alone to roll out their pastry for their own little pies, she moved about the house, cleaning as she went.

"What's that song about?"

"I don't know. My granny used to sing it when I was little, and I hum it whenever I have work to do. It helps pass the time and the chores get done faster." Sorcha smiled, keeping her fingers crossed in the hope the child would respond.

"You sound happy when you sing. But you can't be."

"I am happy. Why wouldn't I be?"

"But you are far away from everyone you know. Why don't you go home?"

Sorcha's good mood vanished. She was silly to think making a pie was going to change this child.

"This is my home now." Sorcha said carefully. Jenny's eyes filled with tears as she made a dash for the door. *Dear Lord, show me a way to get through to that child.*

She worked faster, wanting to get a few chores completed before she had to stop for dinner.

CHAPTER 24

Brian walked slowly to the house. He should have come back to check on the girls at lunchtime, but he was worried about the horse Charlie had brought in. Some people didn't deserve to own animals. He was sorely tempted to feed Charlie to his own pigs.

He stopped at the pump to wash his hands and throw some water over his head. He could do with a bath but that would have to wait until later. He couldn't hear any screaming from the house. That had to be a good sign. He hoped Sorcha and Jenny had fared better today.

Pushing open the door, the scent of baking apples assaulted him. His favorite pie. His stomach grumbled in response. A scene of domestic bliss hit him. His daughters were sitting at the table smiling. Sorcha came in from the kitchen, stopping when she saw him. She put a hand to her hair, leaving a trail of flour across her face.

"Oh. I didn't hear you come in. Dinner is just about ready."

"Thank you. You look happy girls, whatcha been doing?"

"Singing." Meggie lisped getting down from her chair and toddling over to him for a cuddle. He picked her up, sitting her on his knee. "What were you singing?"

"Not me, silly." She hugged him. "Sorra."

"Sorcha not Sorra." Brian corrected.

Meggie giggled "Sorra."

"She can't say Sorcha so that's what she's been calling me. We didn't cook chicken today, so hopefully it's edible."

Brian caught the edge in her voice although she smiled. Deciding to ignore it, he put Meggie back on her chair before retaking his seat at the table.

"I hope you helped your ma."

Jenny looked mutinous. Before she answered, Sorcha intervened.

"Jenny was a great help today. We had a chat this morning and agreed she will call me Sorcha."

Brian caught the pleading look his wife sent him. He was inclined to make Jenny accept the situation but maybe Sorcha was right. Women were better at dealing with feelings and all that stuff.

He took a mouthful of stew. "This is delicious. Thank you." He looked around the room. "The place looks very good. Don't work too hard though. You are not a servant."

Surprise flitted across her face. What did she think he was? *Well, you haven't exactly made it easy for her leaving her alone all the time.* "Is there more?" He held up his plate. She waited, looking at him.

"Pa, say please." Meggie lisped. Sorcha cuddled her and gave her a kiss on the head.

"Good girl, Meggie."

Meggie's smile lit up her whole face at Sorcha's praise. It was infectious.

"I'm sorry. Please may I have some more?" Brian said, smiling too.

Sorcha returned his smile before taking his plate and heaping spoonful's of stew on top. His stomach gurgled appreciatively, causing Sorcha to giggle before holding an apron to her mouth. Her eyes danced.

"Sorry. It's been a while since I ate so well." He tucked into the meal, listening to Meggie chatter to Sorcha. Jenny joined in as well, although not quite as enthusiastically.

The apple pie didn't last long. It was just as delicious as the stew. "You are an excellent cook, Sorcha."

"The girls made the pie but thank you."

Brian bowed his head to Jenny and then to Meggie. "Thank you for my pie." The girls smiled the first real smiles he had seen since losing Abby and Ethan. He pushed thoughts of his loss from his mind. It wasn't fair to bring his grief into this happy moment.

"Sorra, tell us story. Please." Meggie begged as she went over to sit on Sorcha's lap.

"In a minute darling, I have to clear the table first."

"No, you sit by the fire for a bit. Jenny and I will clear up." Brian ignored the angry look his daughter sent him. "It's the least we can do after such a fine meal."

Sorcha looked as if she was going to argue but instead let Meggie pull her over to the fire. She sat before taking the child onto her knee.

"What stories do you like, Meggie?"

"Happy stories." The child hugged closer to Sorcha playing with her hair.

CHAPTER 25

Brian wished he could hear the story but Jenny was making so much noise washing the dishes he had to wait. Once finished, he surprised them all by pulling up the other rocker toward the fire. "Tell us another one."

Sorcha looked even prettier sitting with Meggie on her lap. Her cheeks were flushed, but whether it was caused by the fire or the request, he didn't know. Part of him wanted to believe it was his request.

"Tell us the story of the wicked stepmother." Jenny said, not bothering to keep the spiteful tone out of her voice.

Brian didn't get a chance to admonish her before Sorcha responded.

"You mean King Lir and the swans? The story Ben

spoke about? I don't know if that's a good idea, Jenny, it may scare Meggie."

Brian hid a smile. Sorcha was cleverer than he had given her credit for. While Jenny wouldn't hesitate to hurt her new ma, she idolized her sister and would never put her in harm's way.

"Do you have any happy stories for Meggie? Then later, when she is asleep you can tell us the story of the King?"

Sorcha's stomach turned over as she dragged her gaze away from his. He had such lovely eyes and his voice sent shivers down her spine. She racked her brain for a funny story. She wanted to amuse the children but if she was honest, their father too. Maybe, if she entertained him, he would spend more time with them all. Maybe he wouldn't sleep in the barn. Heat rose to her cheeks. She hoped he blamed the fire.

"Sorra, tell story." Meggie pulled at her shirtwaist bringing her back to reality.

"Do you believe in fairies?" Sorcha whispered to Meggie but made sure her voice was loud enough to carry to Jenny and Brian.

Meggie nodded her eyes glued to Sorcha's.

"In Ireland, there is a special fairy called the leprechaun. He isn't a child and he doesn't have wings. But appears in the form of an old man. It is said he likes to collect gold and will hide it at the end of a rainbow."

"Can we find the gold?" Jenny asked.

Sorcha laughed. "No, love, as the rainbow never ends, does it?"

"So what's the point, then? This is a stupid story."

Sorcha ignored the nine-year-old, instead focusing on Meggie. "If you capture a leprechaun and are nice to him, he will grant you three wishes."

"What's wishes?" Meggie asked, before sticking her thumb back in her mouth.

"Gifts." Sorcha said quickly. "If you wanted three gifts, what would you like?"

"A doll please." Meggie sucked her thumb for a few seconds, her eyes slightly shut. "And candy."

"They're stupid wishes. I would ask for money, you to go away and …."

"Jenny, apologize at once." Brian's harsh tone, combined with Jenny's remark, was too much for Meggie. She started crying loudly. "Sorra, no go." She cuddled closer, her hands holding on so tight, Sorcha winced with pain.

"Meggie, Sorcha isn't going anywhere. It's time for bed."

"No leave Sorra. Meggie stay."

Sorcha held the child closer, if that was possible. She hid her face in her hair not wanting the others to see just how hurt she was. She fought hard to prevent the tears from falling. Brian stood up. "I am really sorry Jenny was so rude, Sorcha. Thank you for the stories."

The door banged shut behind him. Maybe it was better he left, given his temper, but she wished he had stayed. Her hopes for a lovely family evening had gone up faster than the kindling she'd thrown on the fire earlier. *Dear Lord, what can I do to fix this?*

CHAPTER 26

The next morning, breakfast was a quiet affair. Jenny refused to speak to anyone. Her sullen look matched the one on her father's face. Meggie wasn't much better, calling for Sorcha every time she moved out of her sight. By the time they had all finished eating, Sorcha was ready to scream.

Brian left as soon as breakfast was over. He had errands to run in town. She hoped he would ask them to go with him but he didn't. She wished she could go visit Mary but she didn't know where her ranch was. She couldn't just set off walking across the prairie with two children in tow.

The sun beamed in the sky as she hung out another load of washing. In the distance, the creek beckoned her, its blue waters shimmering in the sunlight. She was sick of doing chores and being cooped up inside all the time.

"Come on girls, let's pack a picnic and go down to the creek. We can paddle a bit. What do you say?"

Meggie squealed with delight. Jenny seemed to be fighting a smile but Sorcha wasn't about to let her stepdaughter ruin another day. She was determined to have some fun. They took a blanket to sit on and walked slowly towards the creek. Mindful of Brian's remarks about snakes, Sorcha kept an eye on the ground. Shuddering as she looked at the long grasses, she tried to stop her imagination picturing long snakes just waiting to jump at them. *Snakes don't jump. Do they?*

"Can you swim, Jenny?"

"Pa taught me. He was supposed to teach Meggie too, but he hasn't had time. Can you?"

Sorcha shook her head. "Not much call for swimming in Boston."

"Why? They got the sea there, don't they? I never saw the sea. Is it true the water goes on forever?"

"No but it looks that way when you look out to where the big ships come in. Granny told me about her trip over from Ireland. She wasn't too keen on getting back on a boat once they landed."

"Why did your granny come to America? Why couldn't she stay in Ireland?"

"They had to leave as they didn't have anything to eat. The potatoes suffered from blight." At the questioning look in the child's eyes, Sorcha explained. "It's a disease that causes potatoes to die."

"Could they not live on other stuff? We don't eat that many potatoes. Couldn't they grow vegetables, corn and wheat?"

"In some areas they did but most of the wheat was exported to England. Irish farmers were poor and only had small portions of land on which to grow food. They grew potatoes because you can get a big crop from a small landholding. But when the disease came, all that food source died."

"But why give away food when your family is starving? Pa wouldn't give away our food."

"He would if he had to raise money to pay bills. Irish farmers didn't own their farms. Your pa owns the land your house is built on. In Ireland, the land was owned by landlords who rented it to the tenants. Often, the owners lived abroad and left someone in charge to look after everything. If the farmers couldn't work or sell things to earn money, they wouldn't be able to pay the rent. Then they would get in trouble. So the food was sold."

"So, how come your granny was able to come to America? Didn't it cost a lot of money for the ticket? I want to go to Denver but Pa said the train tickets are too expensive. Denver isn't as far as Ireland."

Sorcha hid a smile. Jenny seemed to have forgotten her vow not to speak to her. She was an intelligent child and her curiosity overcame her dislike. "My granny was lucky. She had some family who had moved to America some years before. They bought her the ticket to travel."

"Wish I had family to buy me a ticket to go see Denver." Jenny kicked at some pebbles, sending them into the water.

"What's in Denver?"

"Thomas Stanton said it had the best circus. His pa took them there last summer. He said they had a fat lady with a beard and an elephant, and some tigers. They even had a man who ate fire but I don't believe that bit." The look in Jenny's eyes belied that statement. "I'd love to see real tigers and other animals. But Pa said no. He always says no." Jenny's kicking became more energetic.

"Maybe he will take you when you are a little older."

"Nope. That won't happen. He doesn't even like us going into Clover Springs."

"Are you hungry? I can hear Meggie's stomach rumbling from here." The little girl was happily building a house with pebbles but looked up when she heard Sorcha say her name. It wasn't yet time to eat but Sorcha hoped to distract Jenny. She didn't want to get into a conversation about all the things Brian stopped his children from doing. Were they even allowed down here by the creek?

CHAPTER 27

As if her thoughts summoned him, they spotted a man coming towards them.

"Pa, are you going swimming?" Jenny raced towards her father. Sorcha watched, her hands twisting. She searched his face for signs of anger. Finding none, she relaxed slightly.

"I got the chores done early so thought we would enjoy the sunshine."

"That was a great idea. Did you pack enough for me?" He grinned at her, causing her heart to soar. "I'm starving."

"Come swimming, Pa."

"Later, Jenny, I want to eat first."

Jenny looked as if she would protest but Sorcha intervened. "Jenny, can you rinse off these dishes for me please?"

Muttering, Jenny took the dishes in one hand and Meggie's hand in the other and walked closer to the creek. Sorcha rose to follow them, but Brian's hand on her arm held her back.

"Let them go. They'll be safe. Jenny knows not to let Meggie too close to the deep water."

Sorcha sat back down but kept her eyes glued to the children. Her skin tingled as his eyes roamed her face but she pretended not to notice.

"Did you punish Jenny for her behavior last night?"

"No. She's hurting. She's only a child and has lost her mother."

"Doesn't give her the right to be rude."

"No, but maybe if we ignore it, she will stop. I want to show her I want to be her friend, not take her ma's place."

Silence greeted her remark. She risked a glance at his face. He was staring at her, a puzzled expression on his face.

"What?"

"Her friend? You are here to be her ma."

"In time, I hope she will see me as someone like that, but for now, I will settle for friendship."

Sorcha stared back at the girls, wishing she could pull up her skirts and join them. As if he read her thoughts, Brian coughed before saying, "Why don't you join them? It's mighty hot."

"I couldn't. It wouldn't be seemly."

"Why? We're married now. I don't think anyone would be shocked if I saw your pretty ankles, do you?"

Pretty ankles? Had he been looking at her? She pushed those thoughts aside.

"Anyone could see me."

His laugh made the girls look toward them. "We are out in the middle of the prairie. Not a soul for miles. Nobody is going to come calling at this time, and if they do, we will see the dust cloud in plenty of time for you to get all respectable again." He scrutinized her so closely she looked at the ground as her ears went pink. "Go on, you are dying to. I can see it on your face." When she didn't move, he leaned closer. "You promised to obey me, Mrs. Petersen."

At that, she moved. Quickly. She didn't want him to know how much his nearness affected her.

He watched as his wife ran down toward his daughters. Shedding her shoes and lifting her skirts slightly, she paddled into the creek. His girls immediately started splashing Sorcha. Her laughter rang out. It was such a lovely sound, as musical as her voice. He found himself comparing her to Abby. There was no way his wife would have gone near the creek. She didn't like water and no amount of persuading could bring her down here to enjoy a picnic.

In fact, she wasn't big on enjoyment. He shouldn't

be thinking that way. Abby had been a good woman. She'd worked hard around the house, making it a home for him and the girls. She'd worked late into the night sewing clothes, quilts and finally some curtains for their room. She was always working, but then, her folks had been that way too.

She wasn't sociable. She preferred to keep her business private. She didn't mind not going into town but she was a good neighbor. The first to offer assistance, if required. But he couldn't imagine her playing with the girls as Sorcha was now. Sorcha looked like a child enjoying the sunshine. She wasn't much taller than Jenny. He watched as she splashed Meggie and Jenny. She didn't seem to realize the water was molding the clothes to her body.

Forcing himself to look away, he swallowed trying to concentrate on another image. His feet itched to walk to the creek and kiss Sorcha. His wife. *But she isn't really? And won't be while you sleep in the barn.* He ground his teeth. It was better this way. Safer. When he'd first decided to bring a woman out here to be a mother to his children, he'd been adamant that was all there was to it. He hadn't bargained on being so attracted to Sorcha.

He lingered for a while longer before realizing his wife would probably be too shy to come back to the picnic when she noticed her clothes. He had chores to do anyway. The work never stopped. He stood up, taking one last look at his family giggling in the stream before setting off back to the barn. *Why did I even go to the creek?*

CHAPTER 28

Sorcha didn't notice when Brian left. She turned to look in his direction but found their picnic area deserted. Her heart sank. Maybe he was angry? He might not approve of her dancing in the water like a child. *But he told me to go into the creek.*

"Come on girls, time to go." Her curt tone got their attention, their anxious looks giving her a lump in her throat. It wasn't their fault she was confused by their father's actions. "Sorry Jenny, Meggie, I didn't mean to sound cranky. I was having so much fun, I lost track of time. We need to get back to start dinner. Your Pa will be hungry."

Grumbling, the girls waded out of the creek toward the bank. Sorcha let Jenny go in front as she picked Meggie up. She almost walked into Jenny who came to a sudden stop.

"Jenny, don't stop like that. I could have hurt you."

Jenny didn't respond, causing Sorcha to look closer. The child was shaking but not with cold. Sorcha followed her gaze which was focused on the ground. On a snake.

She moved Meggie onto her hip and mindful of what Brian had said, moved slowly backward into the creek. "Jenny, stand still. I will be back in one minute. I just want to put Meggie on the bank."

Sorcha moved slowly until she judged she was far enough from the snake not to attract its attention. Then she moved quicker than she ever thought possible. Moving further down the creek, she left the water as quickly as she could. Finding a dry, safe place for Meggie, she set the child down. "Meggie stay here, I will be back in a minute. Do not move."

Meggie sat with her thumb in her mouth. Sorcha was torn between wanting to stay with Meggie to keep her out of danger and going back for Jenny. *Meggie is fine. It's Jenny who needs you.* Praying hard, Sorcha ran back toward the creek until she came close to the terrorized child. Then she walked very slowly, talking softly to Jenny. The child was frozen in place, staring at the snake lying to the right of her foot. The snake wasn't moving. Perhaps it's asleep. Or dead.

"Jenny, move toward me." Sorcha held out her hand

to the child but she didn't seem to be listening. She had to get closer to her.

"Jenny, I'm here. I am going to move to your side. When I take your hand, we are both going to walk away slowly. Okay."

No answer. Sorcha moved closer until she was touching Jenny. "Come on, love. Remember what your pa said, we have to move slowly."

Jenny still didn't move. Sorcha was afraid to pull her in case the jerky movement woke the snake, if it was just sleeping. She hoped it was dead. "Meggie needs you, Jenny. She's up there all alone. She might crawl toward us if we don't move now."

Sorcha watched Jenny's eyes widen, a sure sign her words had met their mark. Holding her hand tightly, she pulled her stepdaughter away from the snake's path. They walked as slowly as possible until Sorcha judged they had put sufficient distance between themselves and danger. Stopping she pulled the child into her arms, her heart beating wildly. Jenny's sobs tore through both of them. "You're safe now, Jenny. Come on, love, let's go get Meggie and go home." She pulled the child behind her as she headed toward Meggie. She was sucking her thumb, watching them with an intense look of concentration on her face.

Sorcha grabbed the baby and together all three of them walked to the picnic blanket. Putting Meggie down for a second, Sorcha packed up as quickly as she could. She draped the rug around Jenny's shoulders as she couldn't stop shaking. Probably shock. Sorcha prayed Brian was home. They made their way slowly toward the house.

"Brian, Brian." Sorcha called, not wanting to alarm him too much but at the same time, she was worried about Jenny. The child was still shaking. Meggie joined in calling, "Pa, Pa."

CHAPTER 29

Hearing his name, Brian rushed out of the barn wiping his hands on his trousers. "Back already, I thought you would…"

His words died as he spotted the trio. Only Meggie looked normal. Sorcha looked even paler than usual, but it was Jenny his gaze focused on. His daughter's eyes had a wild look about them. Moving quickly to her side, he tried to draw her close. "She's shaking. What happened? What did you do to her?"

"Snake, it was at the creek." Sorcha burst out.

"Snake? Did it bite her? Are you hurt, darling? Show Pa."

Jenny shivered violently. Brian's ears roared. He knew it. He shouldn't have risked marrying again. God was angry. He scanned his daughter but couldn't see any angry marks.

"It was asleep, it didn't attack. But she got a fright."

Brian stared at Sorcha. Her eyes blinked rapidly. "Are you sure? Maybe I should take her to town to see the doc, just in case."

He jumped as she touched his arm. "I'm certain. Jenny is fine, although she won't be if we don't get her out of those wet clothes."

Sorcha carried Meggie into the house. Brian scanned his daughter once more before taking her into his arms and carrying her inside. He stoked the fire as Sorcha stripped both girls.

"Can you make her a hot drink? It will help warm her up." Sorcha's voice quivered. Realizing his wife was shivering badly, his stomach clenched. She could get a chill too. "Sorcha, please go and change. You're shaking."

"I'm grand. The girls—"

"Will be fine. Go change now. I will make some coffee."

He stared into her eyes until she backed down. With one last glance at Jenny, Sorcha turned slowly and walked toward her room. The door closed gently behind her.

"Jenny, sit by the fire and mind your sister. I'm going to put on some coffee."

Jenny didn't reply but did as instructed, cuddling her sister on her lap. Making the coffee should have given Brian time to calm down. He heard Sorcha's door open but didn't look at her. His anger, although not aimed at her specifically, wouldn't allow him. He tried to breathe slowly. She came toward him, still shivering slightly. Her eyes were fearful.

"Brian, I'm sorry. I was right behind Jenny. I didn't see the snake. I was distracted."

Before he could answer, Jenny surprised both of them.

"Pa, if you're angry, it's my fault not Sorcha's. She took Meggie out of the water and came back for me. I couldn't move. I was too scar..." Sobs overcame the child, stopping her from speaking.

Sorcha moved quickly to comfort Jenny. She put Meggie on the floor and then pulled Jenny up out of the chair so she could sit first, and pull Jenny down on top of her knee.

"Cry, little one. It will help. It wasn't your fault. It wasn't anyone's fault. We just have to say thanks nothing bad happened."

Sorcha rocked back and forth with the child crushed close against her. She kept rocking until the sobs ceased. After Jenny hiccupped a couple of times, she stopped rocking. "Are you all right now?"

Jenny nodded but still looked worried. "Thank you."

Sorcha kissed the child's cheek and put her arms around her once more. Her racing heartbeat was making her feel dizzy. Every time she closed her eyes, she saw the snake. She wasn't ever going back to the creek. No matter how sunny it was.

She was surprised to see Brian dishing up dinner. She hadn't noticed him doing it. She went to get up but realized Jenny was asleep.

"Jenny, love, it's time for supper." There was no response.

"Let me." Brian picked up his daughter and carried her to her bed.

Sorcha sprang out of the seat and busied herself, getting glasses of water for the table.

"Sit down and eat."

She sat but didn't look at him. Was he still angry? His voice sounded funny.

He sat opposite her, looking at her for a few seconds before reaching across the table. Taking her hand, he looked into her eyes.

"I'm sorry. I shouldn't have blamed you. I know better."

"That's all right," she managed to say but her voice was squeaky. She stared at his strong large fingers enclosing hers, before his voice made her look up.

"No, it isn't. I have seen you with my children. You

wouldn't put them in danger. Today was an accident. You handled it perfectly."

He wasn't looking at her but focused on some distant spot over her shoulder. His eyes had that haunted look she'd seen at the wedding. Somehow she knew it wasn't just grief for his wife and child. Something else bothered him. Deeply.

"I didn't do anything."

"That's not what Jenny said. Anyway, I shouldn't have reacted that way."

She stared at their hands, still joined together. "It's understandable. You've lost so much."

At her words, he took his hand back. Why did she have to say anything? She fidgeted, trying to muster the courage to take his hand again. She looked up to see him staring at the table, his face drawn and pale.

"I should have been there."

He spoke so quietly she almost missed it.

"You can't be with the girls all the time. You have to work."

"I have to protect them."

His growl made her shiver, not with fear but the pain in his voice was too much to bear. She wanted to hug him close but she couldn't do that. *He's your husband. He's a stranger.*

She sat, playing with her hands under the table in

an effort to stop herself from touching him. "You said snakes hid in the grass but there was only mud near the creek."

"Some snakes like the sand. Can you remember what it looked like?"

"A snake."

They exchanged a slight smile.

"Sorry. It was gray but had brown spots on its back. A big head too." Sorcha clenched her shoulders, she didn't want to think of it.

Brian rubbed the whiskers on his chin, his eyes wary. "Sounds like one the Indians call the Massasauga. One bite is fatal."

Sorcha burst out sobbing. She tried to get up to run to her room but he was there. He wrapped his arms around her as she soaked his shirt. The material was coarse against her face but she didn't care. It felt so good to be held. He was so powerful and she clung to that strength. He was stroking her back gently but his touch lit her skin on fire. Her body moved closer to him yearning for more. Lifting her head, she stared into his eyes.

He looked at her hungrily, she saw him look at her mouth before moving back to her eyes. She bit on her lip before standing on her tippy toes and kissing his cheek. At the last minute, he moved and his lips met hers. Groaning, he pulled her even closer as he pressed his lips against hers. He lifted her up so she could wrap her arms around his neck without breaking the kiss. A cry broke through the fog swirling in her brain. A child's cry.

She pushed him away reluctantly. "Brian, one of the children is crying," she said, trying to get her voice under control. It sounded odd – as if she had a sore throat. He set her back on her feet but didn't loosen his hold immediately. Thank goodness he didn't, as she rocked back and forth, unsteady on her feet.

"Sorra, where are you?"

With one last look, she turned and ran to Meggie's bed. When she had settled the child and returned to the kitchen, he was gone.

SHE SAT AT THE FIRE, reliving the embrace. Her whole body heated. *Would he come back? Would he stay? She wanted him to. Didn't she?*

The door opened, allowing a blast of night air into the room. He carried a load of logs over to the fire-place, his face glistening with sweat. "I chopped a load more."

"You were out chopping wood?"

"The log box was almost empty."

They stared at each other for a few seconds until Brian looked away. Then he looked everywhere but at her. *He's uneasy.*

* * *

Brian tried to think of anything other than the woman standing by the fire. She was so beautiful. She smelt good too – fresh and sweet with a hint of something he couldn't quite place. He'd come close to taking her to his room earlier. Too close. That wasn't the plan. *You married her.*

His voice surprised him but not as much as what he said. "I have a lot of work on at the moment." He always had a lot of work to do. Why was he apologizing? She looked puzzled too. "But I am going over to the Sullivan ranch tomorrow. Would you like to come? You could visit with Mary and the girls could get to know Ben better."

She lit up like a Christmas tree, causing sensations he tried to dampen down to run riot through his body. "Thank you. I would love that."

Even her voice affected him. The soft Irish accent combined with the way her eyes danced as she smiled. *She's fragile and weak and not at all suited to life on the prairie.*

"I guess you would like to turn in. Sleep well."

He hardened his heart to the unspoken request in her eyes. Turning on his heel, he marched out the door. Instead of heading into the barn, he strode over to where he had left his ax. Cutting logs would take his mind off his beautiful wife.

CHAPTER 30

The next morning, the sun rose high in the sky. Sorcha was up early and breakfast was ready when Brian walked in. The girls asked questions about Ben the whole way through the meal.

"What is wrong with his leg? He walked funny when we saw him at the station."

"He had polio when he was little. It sometimes leaves you with a limp."

"So he's a cripple for life. How horrible." Jenny said, taking a mouthful of oats.

"We don't define people by their looks or abilities. It's what is inside someone's heart that counts. Ben is a lovely boy. He has had a difficult life but he will be happy now he is living with Mary."

"So all those kids who live in the orphanage are there because no one wants them?"

"Jenny! Apologize to your ma."

"It's okay, Brian." Sorcha turned to smile at Jenny. "Most of the children are there because their parents died. They are too young to look after themselves. Some live there for a while if their parents can't afford to look after them. They may be sick or out of work. There are many reasons."

"So if Pa had died with Ma and Ethan, we would have ended up in a place like that?" Jenny's spoon clattered to the table.

Sorcha stood and went over to his daughter. Putting an arm around her, she said soothingly, "Your pa is right here, Jenny. Don't torment yourself now. You and Meggie are fine. Nobody is sending you anywhere." Sorcha took Jenny's hand. "Well, maybe just out to the pump to clean your hands. You can't go visiting with oats all over you."

The girls ran to the pump while Sorcha busied herself cleaning up.

"You are very good with her. Most women wouldn't have the patience for her antics."

"She is lonely and scared. She cries herself to sleep every night. She needs… oh, never mind."

"No, go on. What does she need?"

"A pa." Sorcha picked up the dishes and walked to the kitchen, leaving him sitting staring at her, his mouth hanging open. How dare she come into his house and lecture him! She didn't know his girls. She couldn't see how much Abby and Ethan meant. He wasn't taking this.

"My girls have a pa. I have to work to provide all this. It doesn't grow on trees you know. You of all people must understand."

"Yes, I do."

"Good."

"I hadn't finished. Of all people, I understand what it is like to lose my ma. I never knew my pa but if I had one, I hope he would have had time for me when I needed him."

"Sorcha, don't..."

"Don't what? Tell you your girls need you. I will do what I can to help your children, but they need more than to see you at meal times. Don't cut yourself off completely. It doesn't cost much to spare five minutes to tell them a story or give them a cuddle before going to bed."

"You have nerve. This is my home and they are my children."

"I thought it was my home now, too."

Sorcha walked out the door banging it behind her. He stared after her.

CHAPTER 31

The trip to the ranch passed in silence. Sorcha was far too angry to make an effort to speak to Brian. Instead, she studied the countryside. She could feel Jenny looking at them but let him deal with his daughter. She held her back straight and struggled to get a grip on her emotions. She was starting to understand why Laura had always cautioned her to hide her feelings. If people didn't know what you were thinking about, they couldn't hurt you.

Mary didn't live far away and soon they were driving the wagon up toward the house. Mary was sweeping the porch and looked really pleased to see them. "I'm so glad you came visiting. I wanted to call on you but…well, newlyweds need time alone."

Sorcha's cheeks flushed and she looked everywhere

but at her husband. Mary didn't seem to notice. She was chatting to the girls.

"Jenny, so nice to see you and look at you, Meggie. Getting bigger every day. Ben will be so happy to see you both. He loves it here, but I think he misses having children around." Sorcha couldn't help smiling. Mary hadn't changed a bit. She talked for longer than anyone else she had met. She barely stopped to take a breath.

"Mr. Petersen, Davy is out on the range but if you would like to come inside I have hot coffee and some cake."

"Please call me Brian, Mrs. Sullivan. I will have coffee later but for now, would you mind if I head into the barn? I know my way around."

"No problem, Brian. Davy is the same, he runs as soon as us women start chatting. Let me know if you need anything."

Sorcha let Brian help her down from the wagon but she didn't look at him. The anger radiated from his body and she wasn't about to cause a scene in front of Mary. She turned toward her friend to find her staring at them, a quizzical expression on her face. Sorcha moved quickly. The last thing she needed was for Mary to start giving Brian a hard time.

She followed Mary into the house, staring around her in awe. It was exactly as her friend had described in her letters. She touched the gleaming table and couldn't help being slightly envious. Mary glowed with happiness. She had found true love and a beautiful house. Now Ben was here, she must have everything she ever wanted.

"Come into the kitchen and meet Mrs. Higgins. I told her all about you."

"Nice to meet you, Mrs. Petersen. Ben told us how you looked after him so well."

"It was nothing. Nice to meet you too, Mrs. Higgins. Mary told me so much about you in her letters."

"All good, I hope." Mrs. H smiled. "Would you like to take coffee into the drawing room, Miss Mary?"

"Not at all. We will stay here in the kitchen where it is warm. You sit down and join us."

"You're the boss, Miss Mary." Both women laughed, leaving Sorcha feeling lonely again. Why was she always on the outside looking in? Shaking her head to get rid of these thoughts, she sat down.

"So, what do you think of Clover Springs, Mrs. Petersen?"

"Please call me Sorcha. I liked what I saw of it, but I haven't had an opportunity to explore it yet. I am hoping to get to town tomorrow. I have to stock up on some essentials.

Mary came back into the room. "The girls are

playing outside with Ben. He's taken them to see his new horse."

"You've given Ben a horse? But, how is he going to ride?"

"You can see for yourself later. Up on the horse, you would never know he had a bad leg. He wants to be just like his pa." Mary beamed with happiness.

Later, they sat out on the porch. Sorcha slapped at another mosquito. She'd be bitten alive at this rate. "Here, try this." Mary handed a small pot to Sorcha. Sorcha sniffed it. The aroma wasn't unpleasant but would take getting used to.

"Indians have used it for years to keep the mossies' away. They also use bear fat but that's a little difficult to come by. Crushed sagebrush works well and smells better."

"I don't know how you do it, Mary. It's like you've always lived here."

"I love it here, Sorcha. I can honestly tell you Clover Springs is my home. Well, in some ways, Galway will always be the home of my heart, but I've found true happiness here. I am sure you will feel the same way soon."

I hope so. Sorcha didn't say anything out loud. She didn't want to face any questions from her friend. If she got a hint Sorcha wasn't happy, she would have the teapot out before she could count to ten.

"This is our garden. It's a little small but we are working on it."

The little garden held all sorts of crops from potatoes, carrots, beets and greens. Mary showed her the root cellar explaining how Mrs. H. stored the excess produce to help carry them through the winter.

"Can she make jelly? Jenny was saying her ma used to boil up the fruit and make jelly for them. I don't know how to do it but I would love to surprise her."

"You're not trying to be Abby, are you?" Mary asked softly.

Sorcha reddened. "No, of course not. But it wouldn't hurt to get the girls on my side and if making them jelly is the way to go well then..."

"I haven't made jelly before. We can learn together. Mrs. H. will show us."

Before they could make any more plans, Jenny came running up.

"Can we go riding today? Ben said he'd let me ride his horse."

"Have you checked with your pa?"

Jenny didn't have to answer, the mutinous look on the girls face said everything.

"Your pa just wants to keep you safe. He doesn't want to lose you."

"Yeah, I know, but it's no fun not being able to do the same thing other children do."

"I know, love. Why don't you go ask him? He's out in the barn anyway." Jenny ran off leaving Sorcha alone with Mary once more.

"He's protective, isn't he?"

"Yes." Sorcha sighed. Was he protective or controlling? She wasn't sure yet.

CHAPTER 32

All too soon, it was time to go home. Jenny and Meggie lay down in the wagon and were soon fast asleep. Worn out by the amount of running and playing they had enjoyed at the ranch. Sorcha stole a look at her husband. He was staring into the distance. How she envied Mary's relationship with Davy. She sighed out loud, causing Brian to look down at her.

"Tired?" He reached out his large hand and brushed her cheek. "You got something on your face. Looks like flour."

"Mmm." Sorcha didn't trust herself to speak coherently. Her stomach fluttered at the sensations his touch had aroused. The wagon hit a rut in the road, causing her to fall sideways.

"Whoa there, don't want you falling out on the dirt.

Townsfolk will think I am mistreating ya." Brian put his arm around her as he pulled her closer. She snuggled against him, trying not to wonder at this change in him.

She stared up at him, and when he looked down, she saw his eyes move to her mouth. Subconsciously, she licked her lips, watching in wonder as his eyes widened. She thought he might kiss her. Closing her eyes, she waited. And waited.

"Whoa there." He pulled the brake on the wagon and jumped down. She felt bereaved at the loss of heat from her side. Why couldn't the journey have taken longer?

* * *

HE CARRIED the sleeping girls into the house as Sorcha trailed behind him. He was pleased his wife was more amenable than when they had first set out for the Sullivan ranch. He watched as she threw some kindling on the fire. It was tempting to take a seat and talk with her. He loved the lilt of her voice as she told the girls stories of her granny. He enjoyed the Irish legends as much as his children, although Sorcha had no idea he was listening. What harm could it do to spend an evening sitting by the fire with his wife? Wasn't that what most married couples did?

You are not most couples. If you let her in, God will punish her too. Enough people have suffered.

"Goodnight, Sorcha." Brian strode off but not before he noticed the look of hurt on her face. He balled his fists but kept walking. It was better she was hurt and alive, wasn't it?

Sorcha stood still for a while after he had gone. She hadn't imagined him cuddling her on the return journey. She thought he wanted to kiss her but maybe he was shy.

Checking that the girls were fine, she wrapped her shawl around her shoulders and took a cup of hot coffee out to the barn. *I am just showing appreciation for his kindness. He didn't have to take us visiting with him.*

Pushing the barn door open, she waited for his acknowledgement but he didn't seem to hear her. She watched as he groomed the horse, taking his time to brush out her coat. He examined each of her hooves, picking out debris with a metal hoof pick.

"I never saw anyone take so much time over one horse." She said softly not wanting to disturb him or the horse.

"Horses work hard and deserve to be treated with respect." He glanced at her before turning his attention back to the horse. "As soon as anyone puts a child on a horse, that child should be trained how to look after the animal."

Sorcha moved closer to one of the horses, allowing it to smell her before she reached out to touch it. "You love these animals, don't you?"

He nodded. "Would you like to brush her down?"

"I don't know how. I mean… you make it look easy but…"

He moved over to where she stood, her heart beating so fast she felt dizzy. Taking her hand in his, he showed her how to groom the horse. "You stimulate the hide like this to remove the dead hair and skin. That way old Daisy here won't go hurting herself on a fence trying to scratch an itch."

Mesmerized Sorcha watched his large hand engulf hers as the brush moved up and down the horse's coat. She swallowed as his hand stilled. He didn't move and she became afraid to breathe. He dipped his head and a few tendrils of her hair caught on his whiskers. Had he just kissed her head? She wasn't at all sure, as it happened so fast. She willed her breathing to still in the hope he might caress her again but the moment was lost. He moved his hand away. "You learn quick. You can finish her while I check on Charlie's horses."

Sorcha was close to stamping her foot with frustration. Any time she thought she was getting closer to her husband, something distracted him. Did he find her ugly? She didn't look like his first wife. Not that the picture she had found had done the woman justice.

Jenny was more than willing to praise the beauty her ma had been. Sorcha clenched her eyes shut. She didn't like the direction of her thoughts. No good would come of being jealous. Particularly of a woman who had lost her life so tragically and so young. She finished brushing the horse as quickly as she could. "Brian, is there anything else you would like me to do before I turn in?"

He stood staring at her, a bridle in his hands. She willed him to say he would follow her in but he didn't say a word. Smothering a sob, she tore her eyes from his and walked out of the barn as fast as her dignity would allow.

CHAPTER 33

Charlie Stanton rode in, hollering for Brian.

"Brian, you best get out here quick."

Hearing tension in Frank's voice, Brian came out of the barn noticing Frank's balled fists at his side. His friend didn't get rankled easy. He looked at him closely before turning his attention to their guest. The cause of Frank's anger was immediately apparent.

"Get off that animal now, you low down..." Brian's tirade was cut short by Sorcha coming out of the house. He shut his mouth so hard his teeth rattled. Charlie paled, stayed silent but dismounted.

"When'd it start?"

"What?" Charlie said.

"When did your horse start riding funny?"

"Couple days back. I figured she would recover by

herself but she seems to be worse. Stupid nag. Should be shot. That's why I came to you. I need a new ride."

"You aren't getting any of my horses."

Charlie went to say something but Brian ignored his attempt to speak.

"You arrogant fool! Did you think she'd get better carrying your fat behind around? If I kicked you in the leg, would walking make it better?"

"No, of course not, but it's different. She's just a dumb animal."

"She ain't the one who's dumb." Frank growled.

Charlie sent Frank a disdainful look. He moved toward the other man but Brian put himself between the two of them.

"A man like you should be banned from owning horses or any other animals. I wouldn't trust you with a rat."

Charlie bristled. "You can't talk to me like that. I came here to provide you with some business. I don't know why I bothered." Charlie moved toward the horse.

"You get back on that animal and I'm gonna pull you off myself." Brian moved slowly toward the horse, ignoring Charlie's outraged face. "Gently girl. I'm not going to hurt you." He held out his hand so the horse could smell him. "Frank, can you take this...gentleman back to town."

"Wait, what about my horse?"

"What horse, Charlie? You said you were going to shoot it. Leave. Now!"

Charlie backed away, his wide eyes staring at Brian. Frank went off, whistling in the direction of the wagon. Brian gave Charlie a look. The man almost ran after Frank. Brian turned his attention back to the horse. He stroked her nose gently. "You're going to be fine girl, just you see."

Sorcha moved closer to Brian. She didn't want to spook the horse but she was curious to see how her husband worked. She watched as he walked around the horse not touching her.

"What are you looking for?"

"I need to be sure it's only her front leg that's the problem. I want her to get comfortable with me too, before I touch where she hurts. Next I'm going to examine each leg."

Sorcha longed to stay and watch but she didn't want to get in his way. She turned to leave.

"You can watch if you like. Just move back. I don't want to risk her kicking you if I accidentally hurt her."

Sorcha moved back and stood watching her husband at work. He lifted each leg gently the whole time murmuring soothing noises to the horse. She watched as he gently pressed each hoof. "They look okay, but I need to check each part carefully."

He walked the mare carefully around the grass circle outside the barn, his face a mask of concentration.

Sorcha saw the horse seemed reluctant to put her right front leg on the ground. Her head kept rearing up every time she took a step.

"See the way she's moving her head. She's a clever lady. She knows that by lifting her head high, she will reduce the amount of weight she is putting on her sore leg. She isn't lame, well, not fully anyway. She needs rest and a proper diet. That idiot Stanton mustn't feed her right. Look, you can almost see her ribs through her coat."

Sorcha didn't move but stood staring at the animal, absorbing what Brian had said.

"It's okay to come forward, she won't hurt you. Let her smell your scent first before you touch her." Sorcha moved slowly to the horse's nose. "That's it. Slowly now. Now girl, this is my wife Sorcha."

Sorcha giggled at the introduction. Who knew her husband would actually speak to animals like they understood him. She rubbed the horse's nose as the animal pushed into her arm.

"I think she smells the apples you been baking with?"

"How did you know I was baking?"

"You smell good."

Sorcha blushed at the look in Brian's eyes. She turned her attention back to the horse. "Can I get her an apple?"

"Why not? It might take her mind off her leg. For a little bit."

Sorcha went to get the apple and returned to find Brian staring at a mark on the horse's leg. "See this. She's got a puncture wound here. We will need to wash it and dress it. It isn't infected, so I don't think it's serious, but I'm not taking any chances. We want her well."

"What will you do with her?"

"Will I give her back to Stanton, you mean?"

Sorcha nodded, stroking the horse's nose.

"I have to. She's his."

"Could you buy her from him? She looks like a nice horse."

Brian laughed but stopped as she glared at him. "I wasn't aware I was so funny."

"Sorry, Sorcha, but you don't know anything about horses. You can't just buy one because they look nice. She isn't a dress."

"I know that. I'm not stupid."

"No, you're not and I'm sorry. I didn't mean to hurt your feelings. I'm sorry."

Sorcha glanced at Brian. He'd apologized and he hadn't meant to laugh at her.

"I have to give her back to Stanton, Sorcha. This is my job. I make sick animals better. I can't take in every mistreated animal I see."

"Why not? We got plenty of space, don't we? The girls would love to have her here."

"Only the girls?" He chuckled as she blushed again. *Why do I keep going red?*

"Let's see if I can make her better first, shall we?"

"Oh, you will. I may not know a lot about animals but I know you do. She'll be fine in no time at all, won't you, Lady?"

"Lady?"

"Yeah, she looks like a Lady, doesn't she?"

Sorcha gave the horse a quick kiss before heading back into the house.

Brian chuckled as his wife walked, make that marched into the house. She was a real city girl, not an ounce of country knowledge in her. She had a kind heart though. She didn't like the idea of the horse being mistreated either. She'd need to toughen up. Living out here in the wilds was no place for the faint hearted. Animals got sick and died every day. Not just animals. He sighed. There was no point thinking about the family he had lost to this land. He had work to do.

He had applied a poultice to the puncture wound just in case there was anything embedded in the wound. Then he had brushed the horse down carefully, all the time trying to keep his temper under control. He didn't want to make the horse nervous. It was a good thing Frank had left Charlie back in town. If the man was standing in front of him, he wouldn't be able to stop himself from hitting him. Had he never learned to use a brush and a hoof pick?

"How's she doing?" Frank asked as he came into the barn.

"She'll be all right so long as she gets enough rest and that leg heals properly. What'd you do with Stanton?"

"I didn't push him off the wagon, if that's what you mean, although I sure was tempted. He's angry though. He was blustering the whole way back about going for the sheriff. He reckons you stole his horse."

The two men laughed loudly just as the barn door opened. Sorcha came in carrying a tray of cookies and hot coffee.

"I thought you hard working men might like a snack."

"Thank you kindly, ma'am." Frank snuck a cookie

from the tray. "You make the best oatmeal cookies I ever tasted."

"Stop saying stuff like that. You make me look bad." Brian joked but his eyes sought Sorcha's to see what her reaction was. He couldn't help it. He wanted to make her smile. She did it readily enough for other people but with him she was shy. As if she was afraid of him. She wasn't, was she? He hadn't done anything to make her fear him. *You haven't done anything to make her trust you either. Sleeping out in the barn when you've got a perfectly good bed indoors. That's for her own protection. Is it?*

Sorcha saw the emotions racing behind her husband's casual glance. He'd been laughing and joking with Frank but stopped as soon as she came into the barn. Was he that uncomfortable around her? No, he couldn't be. It had to be something else.

He seemed to be trying his best to be nice yet as soon as she returned his smile, his face closed over. He was so hard to understand. So complicated. She'd been scared when she heard him shouting at the man from town. True Charlie Stanton had mistreated his animals, but did that mean it was right to shout at him and treat him like a fool? She wasn't sure Father

Molloy would approve. Brian may not like the man but his business depended on his reputation. If he treated every potential customer the way he'd treated Mr. Stanton, he wouldn't be in business for long.

That's none of my concern. My job is to raise his girls and keep the house clean. He's made it obvious he sees you as a housekeeper. If only that was enough. "Frank, are you staying for dinner? I made apple pie." Her husband's business partner looked at her.

"No thank you, ma'am. I got to get back to my place."

She thought she saw pity in his dark brown eyes. She didn't want anyone's pity. Leaving the tray behind her, she walked slowly back to the house.

CHAPTER 34

Sorcha twisted and turned all night. She was going crazy in the house. She loved spending time with the girls but she needed some adult company. She could go into Clover Springs. Brian had shown her how to hitch up the wagon. She needed some stuff from the store. They were low on flour and other foodstuffs. She spent her day cooking and cleaning as usual. When Jenny came in from collecting the eggs, she looked happier. Sorcha decided now might be a good time to bring up the subject of buying new clothes. The dress she was wearing wasn't decent. It nearly came up over her knees.

"How about we go into town tomorrow and see if we can find you some new clothes?" Jenny opened her mouth but before she could speak, Sorcha quickly continued. "You can keep the dress your ma made for special occasions. You don't want to ruin it wearing it every day. Is that a deal?"

Sorcha nearly fell over as the child gave her a quick hug before running toward the barn. Meggie squealed and held out her arms for a hug. "Maybe there is hope for me and your sister yet, Meggie, what do you think?" The toddler grinned and pulled at Sorcha's hair. "Are you going to help me fix dinner for your pa?"

Brian came in earlier than expected. "Something smells good." Sorcha smiled but didn't respond. Who was he kidding? She could serve him boiled rattlesnake and he would still think it smelled good. She said something to Meggie and they both giggled. His heart beat faster. His girls were happy, even Jenny was warming to Sorcha. She was so kind and always smiling, who would be miserable in her company. Even now she was humming as she dished up the dinner. She was good to look at too. *Stop thinking like that and eat your dinner.*

When dinner was finished, she took his plate and

returned with apple pie and cream. The coffee was just as he liked it. The girls chattered about their day. "Sorcha said she would bring us shopping tomorrow, Pa."

Sorcha went quite still, her eyes anxiously darting around the table. She didn't look at him. Was she afraid?

"That's an excellent idea. Sorcha, I have credit at the store so charge up whatever you need."

"I, um, well, I thought I might get Jenny a couple of dresses. She seems to have taken a stretch and the ones she has are a bit short."

Brian smiled, hoping she would return the favor. He had the urge to please her. He liked to make her laugh. They stared at each other, and he fought the urge to pull her closer. Then Jenny interrupted.

"Sorcha likes singing, Pa. She said it made the day pass quicker. Do you think you could play for us tonight?"

His good mood vanished. Pushing back from the table, he said goodnight.

"But Pa, I thought you might stay and read us a story."

"Sorry, Jenny, but I have work to do. Thank you again, Sorcha. See you all in the morning. Be good, girls."

He couldn't look at their faces, the disappointment and hurt burned his soul. Jenny should have known better than to ask him to play. He had no intention of ever playing again.

CHAPTER 35

Sorcha couldn't understand her husband. One minute he was really pleasant to be around. The next, he was grumpier than an old mule. It was almost as if he was afraid to be happy. He didn't know how lucky he was. He had a roof over his head, plenty to eat and two lovely little girls who adored him.

She cleared the table, taking her frustration out on the dishes. The girls didn't understand it either. Earlier they were laughing and joking, now they both looked miserable. Sorcha slammed the cup into the water, spraying it everywhere. He needed to grow up. Sure, he had been through a hard time losing his wife and son but those beautiful girls needed him. They weren't the only ones.

She told the girls an extra-long story about Maeve, Queen of Ireland, and then stayed with them until they were both asleep. Watching them, the thickness in her throat made it hard to breathe. They were so sweet both of them. Sure, Jenny was challenging, but the glimpses of the lovely girl behind the grief were enough to realize she was a good girl. The poor thing was just struggling to cope with the loss of her mother and brother.

She understood loneliness. The pain in her side got worse as she returned to her bedroom. Alone. She had prayed for someone to take her away from the orphanage. Now she wondered if she would have been happier staying there.

After another sleepless night, Sorcha woke up with a headache. *Why did I tell the girls I would take them into town?* Sighing deeply, she got out of bed moving slowly around the kitchen. She didn't speak to Brian. He looked at her with a puzzled expression on his face but she ignored him.

He left as soon as he was finished. The girls spoke softly, as if afraid of disturbing her. She finished her chores quickly before going outside. The wagon was hitched up waiting for her. Brian stood holding the reins. He looked at her expectantly.

"Thank you."

His lips twitched as if he was going to laugh but her glare made him turn away instead. She climbed into the wagon, barely waited for the girls to take their seats and rode off without looking back. Maybe a dose of his own medicine would make him get some sense!

CHAPTER 36

The girls chattered together as they drove into town. Soon they were at the store.

"Good morning, Mrs. Petersen. I am Katie Sullivan, Mary's friend. I was at your wedding but I am not sure you remember me."

"Please call me Sorcha. I feel like I know you already. Mary spoke so much about you at the orphanage."

"Would you like some tea, Sorcha? Daniel can mind the store and I am parched." Katie saw the sorrow in the younger girl's eyes. Her heart lurched as memories surfaced of the way she had felt coming to marry Mr. Cassidy. She was determined to help Sorcha settle in.

"I would, but I have the girls with me."

Katie didn't hide her surprise. "Isn't Jenny going to school? I thought that was why you were in town so early. She missed a lot, you know. She needs to catch up."

Sorcha glanced away from the kind eyes looking at her. What could she say? She didn't want to be disloyal to her husband but it was wrong for him to keep Jenny from school.

"Pa don't want me to go to school. He can teach me."

Sorcha hadn't realized Jenny had heard Katie whispering.

"Of course your pa knows you need schooling, Jenny. What on earth gave her that idea?"

Sorcha gave Katie a look, bringing a flush to the other woman's cheeks. Moving toward the counter, Katie fetched some peppermint sticks. "Jenny, why don't you take Meggie into the sitting room and play a little while we have a cup of tea?" Delighted, Jenny took her sister and the candy, leaving the two adults to walk toward the kitchen alone.

"Does Mr. Petersen really not want the child in school?"

Sorcha shook her head not trusting herself to speak. The tears were threatening again, and she didn't want to cry in front of Katie. Mary had said her friend was kind but still.

"Why would a father not want his child educated? Is it because she's a girl? Some people believe it's not important for females, but I couldn't run the shop if I didn't know my letters and math."

"I don't know, Mrs. Sullivan, I mean, Katie. My husband doesn't say much."

Katie poured the tea, a look of sympathy on her face. "I assume Mary told you I was a mail order bride too. Although it wasn't Daniel who sent for me."

"Yes, she told me the story. It was very romantic."

"Maybe it seems that way now, but living it was a totally different story. I was terrified. I don't mean to pry, Sorcha, but if you ever want to talk, I'm here. I won't tell anyone, not even Mary, unless you want me to."

Sorcha stared, her mouth dry as she battled the temptation to spill her troubles.

"I don't know Mr. Petersen very well but he seems like a fair man. Is he treating you well?"

Sorcha looked at the table.

"Oh, you poor darling." Katie took Sorcha's hand. She lost the battle.

"He's not unkind. He doesn't beat me or starve me but, well…" Sorcha played with her hands. "He sleeps in the barn every night." She whispered.

"Is that all? Oh my dear, he is just being a gentleman. He is waiting for you two to get to know each other first."

"Oh, I'm not complaining about that. I didn't mean

… he is just so unpredictable. Sometimes, he can be very kind and sweet. Other times, he is so angry, he makes me nervous. He doesn't really say anything, apart from telling me what the children can't do. Jenny told me roast chicken was his favorite meal and he planned to kill the hen the night I arrived, so I did and I cooked it and it was his best layer. Then Jenny nearly got bitten by a snake when I took her to the creek. Yesterday, well I don't know what I did wrong yesterday. I think he's sorry he married me." Sorcha burst out before the tears flooded down her cheeks. Katie held her in her arms but she couldn't stop. She sobbed her heart out until she couldn't cry anymore.

"I'm so sorry. What must you think of me?"

"I think you are a young woman thrown into a situation that is far different from one you dreamed about. Mary told me you were a romantic. You saw the best in everyone and life was all roses."

"She said that?" Sorcha hiccupped. "My granny used to tell me stories about Ireland. I should have known better than to believe in happily ever after. I grew up listening to stories about doomed lovers. Granny's favorite was the story of Fionn MacCool when he was an old man. Grainne, his very young fiancée, fell in love with Diarmuid. They eloped but didn't live happily ever after. Fionn chased them down and Diarmuid died. I should have listened. Granny was trying to tell me that life wasn't about happy endings."

"I don't think things are that bad, are they?" Katie's smile was warm but her eyes were wary.

Sorcha didn't answer the obvious question. She continued talking as if Katie hadn't said anything. "When I was hungry or the other kids were mean, she used them to take my mind off things. She told me over and over again that life never works out happy, yet I believed I could be different. I am so stupid."

"Everyone wants a happy ever after, Sorcha. My mam used to say every cloud had a silver lining. It's only been a few days. You and Brian have to get to know one another. His wife Abby and their little boy haven't been dead that long."

"I know he just wants someone to keep house and look after the girls. He was crystal clear in his letter. I was stupid to think he meant otherwise."

"People don't always know what they want. Sometimes what they think and what God has in mind for them are two totally different things. If you want some advice, I would say start the way you mean to go on. You know school would benefit Jenny. She would be happier and it would help get over the loss of her mam. Take her to see Miss Freeman. She's the new teacher. She hasn't been in town long either. She lives with Mrs. Grey, so I am sure she would welcome some younger company."

"Mrs. Grey? Isn't that the lady who doesn't like us Irish?"

"Mrs. Grey is the reason I am still alive. She saved my baby too. I wouldn't say we are best of friends now but I think she is mellowing." Katie smiled but her eyes were full of sadness. "There is a reason why Mrs. Grey believes so poorly of the Irish but that is not my story to tell. Oh my, is that the time? Daniel will think I got lost."

Sorcha stood up so quickly, she knocked the tea cup over. "I'm sorry. I'm not normally clumsy.

"Don't worry. It's not broken. No harm done."

"Come downstairs, Jenny and let's see if we can find you a new dress. Mrs. Shaw dropped off some dresses yesterday. Her granddaughters have outgrown them." Katie gently picked up baby Ella who was still sleeping. She snuggled closer to her mother's shoulder. Katie held her other hand out to Jenny.

"I don't want someone else's old clothes. I have a dress."

"Jenny Petersen, do not speak to Mrs. Sullivan like that. What do you say?"

"Sorry, Mrs. Sullivan."

Sorcha warmed at the look of approval Katie shot her before she turned her attention to Jenny. "If you had let me finish, Jenny, I was going to say, one of the dresses had never been worn. I think it is just your size as well. Shall we have a look?"

Jenny flushed slightly before saying "yes please" softly and taking Katie's hand as she led her downstairs.

CHAPTER 37

Sorcha picked up Meggie, taking her to the sink to wash her sticky hands and face. Then she quickly followed Katie downstairs. She came to a sudden stop at the transformation in her step-daughter. The new dress highlighted her coloring, making her look prettier than ever. "Oh my. Wait till your pa sees you."

"Do you think he will like it?" Jenny turned this way and that trying to see her reflection in the window.

"I think he would love it but should you keep it for church on Sunday."

"No point, we don't go to church no more. Pa told Reverend Timmons it was the chores that kept him home. But it's not that. God took Ma and Pa doesn't like him anymore."

Sorcha knew Jenny had no idea of the shock her words had brought on the women before her.

"Did Mrs. Shaw bring in any other dresses in Jenny's size, Katie?"

Katie pulled out three but they discarded two of them almost immediately. The dull patterns would do nothing for anyone's mood. The third one, while worn, would be perfect for day to day wear.

Katie was still rummaging, and with a whoop of delight, she produced some garments for Meggie. "Oh, look. She will be a cutie in this one."

Sorcha charged her purchases to her husband's account. It was time to put her mark on this family.

They walked down the boardwalk in the direction of the pretty little school house. She knew from Mary's letters it was a recent addition to the town. The school bell rang just as they arrived. They were nearly knocked over by children flying out of the school. Sorcha saw a young stern looking woman at the top of the steps. She approached with caution. People in authority had always intimidated Sorcha, even if they were only a few years older.

"Miss Freeman? My name is Sorcha Matth…. I mean Petersen. This is Jenny and her sister Meggie. I was wondering if I could speak to you about Jenny returning to school."

"Pa won't like this at all." Jenny kicked the ground.

Sorcha ignored both the child and Miss Freeman's raised eyebrows. "I believe schooling is important for all children. I'm sure you agree, Miss Freeman."

"Nice to meet you, Mrs. Petersen. Why don't you come inside out of the sun? Jenny can show me if she knows how to read and write."

"I ain't stupid. Of course I can read and write. I used to go to school every day. Ma… my real ma made me." The fight had gone out of the child's tone as she turned away from the adults. They exchanged a look before Miss Freeman bent down. Putting a finger under Jenny's chin, she forced her to look up. "We don't use the word ain't."

The teacher's tone, while kind, was also firm. *She won't take any nonsense.*

"I don't believe any child is stupid. Some have more learning than others but everyone has a gift. Now why don't you take a reader and show me where you are at?"

Sorcha waited while Miss. Freeman tested Jenny. She could see the child was enjoying the attention, regardless of what she said about not wanting to go to school. She had to convince Brian he was wrong. Children needed an education but also time with other children to learn, play and just be… normal. Once Miss. Freeman was finished testing Jenny, the child ran outside to play taking Meggie with her, leaving Sorcha alone with the teacher.

"Your daughter is very bright."

"Thank you. She's my stepdaughter. Her ma and brother were killed last year. In the floods."

"Oh my. I'm so sorry." Tears filled the teacher's eyes. Sorcha looked away to give the lady a few minutes to compose herself.

"My husband is protective. Understandable, I suppose, but I can't see what harm she could come to in school. Education is important. Especially for girls."

Miss Freeman took her arm as she led her out of the school. "I am so pleased to hear you say that. Far too many people believe a woman has no requirement for learning. But with attitudes like yours, maybe that will change. I will look for Jenny on Monday."

"She'll be here. Good afternoon, Miss Freeman."

CHAPTER 38

Sorcha called Jenny and they set off for home. The girls were silent allowing her time to think of what she would say to Brian. She ran the conversation over and over in her head but nothing sounded right. As they rounded the bend and saw the house in the distance, Jenny spoke softly.

"It's no use, Sorcha. Pa ain't going to let me go to school."

"You want to go, don't you?"

"More than anything." Jenny's eager eyes stared back at Sorcha.

"I will speak to your pa when the time is right. Don't say a word."

The girl blanched. "You mean lie…to Pa?"

Sorcha fidgeted with the reins. "No, of course not."

She modulated her tone. "I just want to pick the right time to discuss it. Let me try please."

But she didn't get a chance. As soon as they arrived back at the house, Brian walked out of the barn.

"Sorcha, I have to go to Denver. Cal Sutton, one of my richest clients, sent one of his boys for me. He arrived a few hours ago but I had to wait on you to come back."

"Sorry. I got delayed visiting with Katie and baby Ella."

"No need to apologize. You weren't to know. You will be safe here. Frank said he will call by every couple of days to check on you."

"Could we not stay with Mary?" Sorcha regretted asking as soon as she spoke.

"I don't like being indebted to people. The Sullivan's have been good to us. You will be fine here. There is sufficient food and you can hitch up the wagon if you need to get to town."

Sorcha smiled despite herself. She was proud of what she had learned in the short time she'd been Brian's wife. Not his real wife. He still slept in the barn.

She stood watching as he readied himself for the trip. He said goodbye to the girls, giving both of them a big hug. They cried but the promise of a present cheered them up no end.

Finally, he was ready to go. She stood waiting to see if she would get a hug too. Her heart beat so rapidly as he came closer, she thought she would faint. Biting her lip, she gazed up at him. "Take care, Sorcha. See you soon." He bent as if to kiss her but at the last minute he touched his lips to her forehead. She clenched her fists, as the desire to pull him down into an embrace almost overtook her. Then he was gone.

Gathering the weeping children to her, she walked slowly back to the house. The day passed slowly. The children behaved badly. She was hard pushed to keep her temper in check. Finally, they fell asleep and she collapsed on the bed, thinking sleep would come easy.

But it didn't. And the next few days dragged by slowly as well. Soon it was Monday. Sorcha hitched up the wagon and drove Jenny to school. Jenny wasn't happy. She wanted to walk, not take a ride in the wagon. After some hesitation and arguments from Jenny, Sorcha agreed to let her walk home from school.

She wished Brian could see how proud and confident Jenny looked as she walked up the school steps. But maybe it was best he didn't. He might not have agreed with her decision. Well, he wasn't here. She was in charge of the girls now.

CHAPTER 39

Something woke Sorcha. She listened to the night sounds, her heart racing. *You are being silly. It's not the first time you've been alone in the house.* She heard the barn door squeak. Looking out the window, she could only see the shadow of the building. The sky was overcast. *Why couldn't the moon be clear and give me some light?*

Maybe Brian was home. He was probably hungry. Rising, she put a blanket around her shoulders and headed out toward the barn. She called his name but he didn't answer. *Maybe he didn't hear me.*

She pushed the door open but the barn was in darkness. A horse nickered but it wasn't a sound of distress. Turning, she headed back toward the house. Must have imagined it.

But then she heard the cry. Shivers went down her back. It sounded like a baby. She whirled around, her eyes getting used to the dark. She could make out a couple of shadows.

"Who's there?"

Nobody answered. She took a step toward the figure. They must be desperate to be traveling in this weather with a baby.

"Please don't be frightened. Just tell me who you are. My name is Sorcha Petersen."

"Nandita. I sorry. I had to take shelter for the baby. We no touch anything. Will leave at first light."

Sorcha gasped, her fear reflected in the chocolate brown eyes staring back at her. The girl looked half-starved and had been hit quite recently if the bruising on her face was anything to go by. She held her baby close to her chest. There were two other children standing behind her.

Sorcha spoke without thinking. "Please come into the house. The fire is warm and I have some stew on the stove. You look frozen, not to mention hungry."

The girl didn't move.

"Please. It will be okay. My husband isn't here. It is just us." Sorcha spoke slowly, wondering how much English the woman understood given her broken speech.

The Indian seemed to consider Sorcha's plan

before saying something to the children. They moved slowly towards Sorcha. She had to resist the urge to gather them to her. They looked so frightened.

"Come on, little ones. We will be warmer in the house."

CHAPTER 40

The sad little group followed Sorcha as she made her way back to the house. She poked the fire, causing the blaze to throw more heat into the room. "Please sit. Would you like some coffee? I can make hot milk for the children."

"We will not take your food."

"Please do. We have plenty."

The children looked toward Nandita, their eyes huge. She sighed before giving her assent. Sorcha poured some milk into a pan before putting it on the stove to heat. She also put some biscuits into the warmer before checking the stew. It was still warm.

She worked quickly as the new arrivals huddled around the fire. Soon she had plates of steaming food set out on the table.

"Would you like me to hold the baby while you eat?" She smiled at the Indian girl. When she hesitated, Sorcha moved slowly toward her. "You need to eat. Your milk will dry up if you don't and your baby will starve."

"Thank you." The girl said formally before handing over her precious bundle. Sorcha was astonished to see the baby staring back at her. He was so little but he didn't seem afraid.

"What's his name?"

"Mohe. And this is Ama and Salali."

Sorcha smiled at the little girls but they just gazed back at her.

"I am sorry. They are very, how you say it, shy. They no see white woman before."

"I haven't met an Indian before." Sorcha laughed softly before looking at Nandita. "Your face looks very sore. My granny always told me to cut a potato in half and rub it over a bruise. Would you like to do that?"

Nandita touched the side of her face gingerly. "Tomorrow I will collect some herbs. For now, I will try the potato. What is granny?"

Sorcha tried but couldn't stop the giggle. "My granny was my mother's mother. She came from Cork in Ireland. To be honest, I think the potato was used to cure everything, not just bruises. I don't know how much help it will be but it won't hurt. I can make you some willow bark tea if you are in a lot of pain."

Tears filled the Indian's eyes. She looked away, obviously trying to compose herself. A few seconds passed. Sorcha wished she could think of something to say to make the girl feel better.

"You are very kind to feed us like this. I sorry we took shelter in your barn. I didn't… I mean, I wasn't sure where to go. We will leave tomorrow."

"Please don't leave. Stay a few days until you recover. My husband is away. It is only the girls and me. It gets lonely out here. You need to rest. Please."

Nandita stared back at Sorcha. She thought she was going to say no, but eventually, the girl shrugged. "We will stay for one more day then we must leave. I have to find other members of my tribe."

Sorcha didn't want to ask about her husband. Was he the one who had bruised her face?

Once everyone had eaten, the children started yawning. "You are welcome to sleep here in front of the fire if you wish?"

Nandita smiled. "Thank you. But what about your daughters? Will they not be frightened?"

Sorcha hadn't considered that. "Jenny is a sensible girl. She will understand. I am usually up before them, so I don't think it will be an issue."

The Indians had turned in for the evening, and

Sorcha returned to her bedroom. She pulled the covers back up on Meggie, who had crawled into her bed the first night Brian left for Denver. She refused to sleep alone since. Sorcha turned down the light and slipped into bed. Shivering slightly, she said a silent prayer to keep everyone safe.

CHAPTER 41

The next morning Sorcha was surprised to find Nandita up and preparing breakfast.

"I hope you don't mind. You were so kind to us last night."

"But you are my guest. You should be taking it easy."

Nandita smiled back. "I slept in front of a warm fire with a full belly. I am taking it… easy." Nandita stumbled over the English words but she was catching on quickly.

They smiled at each other before Jenny's gasp interrupted them. Sorcha moved toward her step-daughter, putting a reassuring hand on her shoulder. "I asked Nandita and her family to take shelter with us."

"Your face looks very sore." Jenny said staring.

"Sorcha knows ways to make it better. She's very good at doctoring, aren't you?"

Sorcha couldn't help smiling at her stepdaughter's praise. She hugged the girl before setting the table. They had a very enjoyable breakfast, teaching the Indian family how the white people ate. Sometime later, Sorcha spotted a young Indian boy standing on the rise staring down at the house. She called Nandita. "I think someone is looking for you? Do I need to go get Brian's shotgun?"

Nandita shielded her eyes as she looked in the direction Sorcha had pointed. "It is Little Beaver. He is the son of my husband's first wife. He means me, us, no harm."

"But his father..."

"He hates his father too. Sleeping Bear doesn't believe he has what it takes to be a real brave."

"He's only a child. I do not like your husband." Sorcha said, so vehemently Nandita laughed out loud.

"Sorry but you should see your face. It is all screwed up like an animal who ate a sour berry."

Nandita beckoned to Little Beaver to come closer. She spoke to him in her own language. Sorcha didn't understand one word, but it was obvious Little Beaver wasn't happy. He kept making hand gestures. Nandita frowned.

"What is it? The boy seems upset."

"He says Sleeping Bear is still ill and it is time for us to run away. He thinks we can reach safety before his father recovers to ride after us."

"So why don't you go? Do you not think he is right?" Sorcha's stomach clenched with worry. Not just for her friend but for the little girls she looked on as her own. She didn't want an angry Indian brave putting their lives at risk.

"I cannot move quickly, the little ones slow me down. I must rest for a day or so to recover my strength. Then we will find shelter with the nearest tribe."

Nandita spoke to Little Beaver again. Judging by her sharp tone and his sullen face, they didn't agree on the plan of action. Nandita turned to Sorcha. "Can we stay one more day and night?"

"Yes, of course. We will make some food for you to take with you. The tribe might be more accommodating if you bring them some cakes."

Nandita grinned. She said something to the boy and he smiled too. "Many Indians have sweet tooth. This is a good idea."

"Works with white men too." *Sometimes.* Sorcha wished it was that easy to find the way to Brian's heart.

It was such a lovely day they raced through their chores and took a picnic outside. Meggie played with the two young girls while Mohe gurgled in his mother's arms. Little Beaver and Jenny chatted some distance away.

"Pa saw a light and it wasn't a candle." Jenny gave Little Beaver a dirty look. His face remained impassive. "He said it was electricity. It was in Denver." Jenny pointed at Sorcha. "Shortly before she came here."

Nandita looked at Sorcha but now wasn't the time to answer the questions the brown eyes held. She corrected Jenny's behavior. "Jenny, don't be rude to our guests please."

"Little Beaver didn't believe me. He thought I was lying."

"I did not say you speak with forked tongue. I said I have not heard of this thing you call a light. It is like a fire but inside a glass."

Jenny nodded. "You have oil lamps right?"

"What are oil lamps?" The boy stumbled over the foreign word.

"Don't boys know anything?"

Sorcha exchanged a look of amusement with Nandita. "Jenny, why don't you take Little Beaver into the house and show him the oil lamps? I don't know what Indians use for light after it falls dark. Perhaps he has never seen a lamp before."

Jenny stood but the look she gave Little Beaver said

it all. Sorcha had to turn her face away so the boy wouldn't see her amusement. She didn't want him to think he was being made fun of.

"I am sorry, Nandita. Jenny is quite straight speaking at times."

"She does not like you coming to live here?"

Sorcha pulled at the threads in her skirt. "No, she thinks I want to take her ma's place. I don't know if she will ever accept me."

"It is the same in our tribe when the man takes a second wife. Often there is jealousy. Little Beaver was not happy when I took his mother's place but she wasn't dead. Not then." Nandita looked down taking a few seconds to compose herself. "But now we are good friends. It will be the same for you with time and kindness. She has sad eyes. She needs you."

Sorcha hoped the girl was right but every time she thought she had made some progress with Jenny, something happened to disillusion her. Like the day she took the curtains down to wash them. Jenny had accused her of ripping all traces of Abby from the house. If only it was as easy as stripping down curtains. But the woman was everywhere. The children weren't the only constant reminders of her presence. There was also the distance between herself and Brian. He was her husband but in name only.

CHAPTER 42

The next few days passed quickly. Every day, Nandita said she would leave but Sorcha begged her to stay. She enjoyed her company and hated the thought of being alone with the girls at the homestead.

The children ran squealing as she chased them around the yard. They giggled and screamed for mercy when she caught and tickled them. They all laughed so much, most of them ended up crying. Sorcha saw tears of laughter on Nandita's face too.

"They are so innocent. Why do children like this grow up to become people who hate?"

"I don't know." Sorcha shrugged. "Maybe it's because we keep them apart. Back in Ireland, the Protestant and Catholic children are not allowed to play together. You can't learn about someone else's way of doing things if you never spend time together. You grow up frightened, and fear drives people to do horrible things."

"I long for the day my people can wander the land free again. The buffalo will be many and our tribe will be happy."

"Do you think that day will ever happen?"

"I don't know. I hope so."

"Let's not think about that now. I'm starving and I guess the kids are too. Why don't we have our picnic under that big tree over there? It will give shade to the younger ones."

The children followed them still laughing. They helped the adults set out the food. Peace reigned as everyone ate their fill. Sorcha's heart melted at the little brown faces whose eyes popped out of their head. They grabbed for whatever foods took their fancy. Jenny and Meggie stared at them for a few minutes before following their example.

"Don't you get enough to eat?"

Nandita shook her head. "Our men used to hunt but since the railroad and the white man came, it is different. The buffalo have left. We still gather fruit and berries but it is more difficult to find meat. The children are hungry. The adults too, but it is harder on the young."

"You are never going hungry again." Sorcha was

determined her new friend would be better off. "As long as we have food, you are welcome to share."

"But your husband, he is coming. He may not like this." Nandita said.

Sorcha looked where Nandita had pointed. *Brian was back*. Her stomach heaved but she tried to keep her voice calm. "Leave him to me. He is a kind man." *Well, sometimes and only to his animals*. But Sorcha wasn't going to dwell on that now. She tried to walk toward Brian but her feet refused to move. Instead she waited for him, rubbing her sweaty palms down the side of her dress.

"What are you doing? With them?"

"Having a picnic." Sorcha tried but failed to stop her voice from shaking. Anger radiated from him, his face stony, his large fists clenched at his sides. Glancing at Nandita, she found a reflection of her own fear. The children had stopped playing. Everyone was looking at Brian.

"You know what I mean, Sorcha. I told you my children were not to be around savages."

Sorcha stiffened her spine. "They aren't. Nandita is my friend and these are her beautiful children. Jenny and Meggie are happy, for once. Can't you see that?" *Please don't make a scene. Don't ruin it for everyone.*

Brian addressed Nandita. "Get off my land. My

wife had no business inviting your kind here. Leave now."

"Or what?" Sorcha stood in front of her husband, hands on hips. Her heart was beating wildly. Just how far would he go?

"Don't push me, Sorcha. If they don't leave now, I won't be responsible for what happens next."

Nandita's sharp intake of breath was like a red rag to Sorcha. "So you would turn your gun on a woman and her children? What sort of man are you? Your parents must be very proud." As soon as she spat out the words, she regretted them. The pain in his eyes was evident to see. He seemed to deflate right in front of her.

"Finish your picnic, then leave. Do not come back. Sorcha, take my children home."

"But…"

"Now Sorcha."

He stalked off before she could say anything else. She stared after him willing him to change his mind but he didn't. Aware of the silence behind her, she turned around to find the children huddled together. Tears streaming down the faces of the little ones. The older ones looked just as terrified. Going toward them, she held her arms out and gathered them into a hug.

"Please don't be scared. You are safe here." But

were they? Her husband hated Indians. She hadn't known that. Well, it was hardly something to come up in everyday conversation. But he wouldn't harm a child, would he? She sent the children away to play and began helping Nandita pack up.

"I am so sorry. I promised you shelter. I didn't know he would react this way."

"It is not your fault. Your man is in pain. His eyes have deep shadows."

"Never mind him. What will you do?"

"We will return to my people. It is time. Thank you for your kindness. You are a true friend to Nandita and her little ones."

CHAPTER 43

Sorcha, Jenny and Meggie stood waving as they watched the little group walk away over the prairie. "Why did they have to go? I hate Pa."

"Don't speak about your pa like that, Jenny. He has his reasons."

"They were my friends. Now I am left to play with Meggie again. It's not fair."

"I will talk to your pa, Jenny. But don't say anything to him now. You will only make it worse."

Together, they walked slowly back to the house. There was no sign of Brian.

Later that evening, when the girls were in bed, Sorcha headed to the barn. Brian hadn't come in for dinner and was obviously avoiding her. Bracing herself, she opened the barn door. She knew he had heard her but he didn't stop grooming his horse. How can a man so kind to animals be so horrible to people?

"Brian… I am sorry, I…"

"Go to bed."

"No. I want to know why you behaved like you did."

"Why? What came over you to bring those, those…?"

"People?"

"Sorcha, they aren't people. Do you not know what they do to the whites?"

"Those children and Nandita have done nothing to anyone. They are the victims. They are dying from starvation and disease."

"They brought it on themselves. They should have moved west like they agreed."

"How dare you speak about people as if they were cattle? Why should anyone give up their homes just to accommodate strangers coming into their land? Look what that did to Ireland."

"This isn't Ireland, Sorcha. It's not the same."

"It's exactly the same. The Indians lived here first, and then people like us came and set up homes without even asking. We killed their source of food, we brought in the illnesses they have never seen before and then, when they try to protect what is theirs, we kill them."

"It's never that simple!"

Sorcha stepped back, the anger in his face frightening her as much as it had the children earlier.

"Sorry. I didn't mean to shout. But life is not black and white, Sorcha. I do not want those Indians on my land again."

"I thought this was my home too."

"It is."

"No, it isn't. If it was, then I would be free to bring home my friends and have a picnic. That is all we were doing today. Having fun. You should try it sometime." Sorcha swallowed hard. She wasn't going to let him see her cry. She had some pride. "I best get back to my chores before you kick me off your land too."

"Sorcha, wait. You're being childish."

She stormed back to the house, banging the door behind her. Of all the mule-headed, inconsiderate men she had ever met, how had she fallen in love with the biggest one of all?

Love? She didn't love him. She hated him. If it weren't for Jenny and Meggie, she would leave tomorrow. *But where would you go? Nobody wants a love child.*

Sorcha flung herself on the bed, sobbing. If only there was someone who would listen to her. Her sister. If she could find her, they could be a real family. But where would she start looking? It was hopeless.

She could no more leave Jenny and Meggie now, than she could go work for Mr. Shepherd. This was the life she chose. There was no going back now.

CHAPTER 44

The door banging echoed across the yard. Stroking the horse, the tears fell unheeded down his face. He hated the fear in her eyes when she had looked at him. Did she think he was a monster?

Well, he was, wasn't he? The son of one anyway. Didn't the good book say the sins of the fathers followed through? Maybe that's why God had taken Ethan and Abby – to punish him.

He opened his eyes trying to dispel the image he had come across earlier. Why had he gone to investigate the laughter? He wanted to be part of it. That hope had died as soon as he came over the top of the hill and saw the scene below him. The nut brown bodies running around his children had frozen his heart. What were they doing? He had started running, yelling for them to leave his kids alone before he realized they had just been playing. It was so innocent yet it wasn't. Despite what Sorcha had said, those kids would one day be full of hatred. So bad they would give their right hand to kill his family.

They were full of hatred? What was he? He had threatened a bunch of youngsters and their mother who stood half his size. Was she even their mother? She looked younger than Sorcha. She had stared back at him, her eyes not reflecting his hatred but full of pity and something else.

Understanding perhaps? How could she understand how he felt? Nobody could. Not even Abby knew the full story. But she was dead. Drowned and it was all his fault. He'd only insisted on going to church because his bad dreams had frightened him.

He worked through the night, telling himself the mare needed his attention just in case her foal came early. The sun had barely risen in the sky when he heard her voice.

"Mr. Petersen, may I please speak with you?"

Brian looked up to find the young Indian girl standing in front of him. She stared back at him but her hands were shaking. *She's terrified.*

"What do you want?" he said, his tone gruffer than he intended.

"Say sorry. Please do not blame your wife. It was my fault."

"Sorcha knows how I feel. She should obey me. She is my wife."

"Yes, she is. You are a very lucky man to have such a kind, honorable, hardworking wife. There are many braves in my tribe who would envy you."

"One of your braves wants my wife?"

Nandita giggled. "Sorry, Mr. Petersen, for laughing. They do not want a white woman, but an Indian woman like Sorcha."

He grunted, hoping she would take it as a dismissal. Instead, she stood there staring at him.

"What?"

"I just wonder why you hate us so much. Did my tribe do something to you, Mr. Petersen?"

"Go away. I don't have to justify myself to you."

"I am very sorry for the loss of your first wife and your son. I was told they died in the floods. We lost many too that winter. But we do not hate those around us. We will not come to your property again. It pains me to say this as Sorcha is a good friend. Please treat my friend as well as she deserves."

The girl turned and walked away slowly. He sat, as his legs would have given way otherwise. He did treat Sorcha well, didn't he? She had plenty to eat, warmth, a home and a family. Everything she wanted. Well, perhaps not everything, but as much as she could have expected given their situation. She was happy. She smiled a lot and she had friends in Clover Springs. She didn't need any more friends did she?

CHAPTER 45

The barn door opened again. Surely the Indian hadn't come back. He rose to find his daughter staring at him. He opened his arms, welcoming her for a hug but she didn't move. Her anger hit him in waves.

"Why do you hate the Indians, Pa?"

Brian rubbed at the back of his neck. He didn't want to have this conversation. "I don't hate them. I just don't want them around you. They could be dangerous."

"Nandita wouldn't hurt me. The rest are just children."

"Children grow up."

"But they never hurt us before, Pa. Why would they do something now? Has this something to do with Grandpa?"

A cold sweat covered Brian. "Who told you about Grandpa?"

"Ma showed me old pictures of him. He had his uniform on. He looked smart. It was taken before he left for the war."

Brian stared at Jenny but it wasn't her face he saw. It was his ma's. She was holding him tight, to stop him from running down the road after his pa marched off to war. He'd thought that was the worst day of his life. He was wrong. The worst one was when Pa had come home. He turned away from Jenny.

"Pa, what's wrong. Why are you crying?"

"Crying? I got a piece of dirt in my eye. Don't you have chores to do?"

"Well, yes, Pa, but I thought…"

"You thought you would get out of them by talking to me. I don't have time for lollygagging out here. Now go get those chores done and then read your bible. I haven't seen you with the good book in your hands for some time now."

"You would if you ever came in the house."

Brian stood still. "What did you just say?"

"Nothing, Pa." She ran and he didn't stop her. Where had it all gone wrong? He'd once had a happy family and now it was gone. Just like it had disappeared before.

Brian sat as the memories assailed him. His ma's

joyful face as the man she loved came back from the war. The joy didn't last. The man who returned may have looked like Pa but that was it. This stranger drank heavily and was bad tempered. He took the switch to his children with increasing regularity. He left only when he hit Ma. Brian had been Jenny's age. He'd come back from school early to witness his pa strike his ma, knocking her to the ground. He had run at his father, beating him as hard as his little fists could. "Go away, go back to the war. We don't want you here. We don't need you. We hate you. I wish you were dead."

He'd gotten his wish. His pa was found a few days later. He needed to get away, ride off his anger and frustration, before he turned into his pa and hit his children.

CHAPTER 46

He slowed the horse as he neared home. "Sorry, Jackson. I guess we both had to run it out of our system." The horse snorted but Brian was distracted by sounds coming from the house. The door opened, framing Sorcha in the light, her shawl wrapped tightly around her shoulders. He dismounted, waiting to see if she would walk toward him.

"Jenny went to bed crying. She said you were upset. She doesn't know what she did to make you so angry." Sorcha stared at him with such a distasteful expression on her face, he wanted to get back on the horse and gallop away.

"I'm sorry. She didn't do anything." Brian said softly. "Go back to the house where it's warm."

"I'm warm enough. What happened to make you

this way? You are so kind to your animals yet you terrify your own child."

Brian tended to his horse, playing for time. What could he say? Nothing justified upsetting his child. Sorcha stood watching him. The silence continued with only Jackson's snorts interrupting.

"Tell me, Brian. Make me understand. I don't think you are a cruel man. You couldn't treat your animals the way you do if you were. You behaved like a monster. I cannot live with that person. Neither can the girls. What happened to make you like this?"

Brian continued rubbing down the horse. He was so ashamed for the way he had treated Jenny, never mind Nandita and her children. He took so long thinking, Sorcha let out an exasperated sigh before turning away from him. She only took one step before he started talking.

"Ma died soon after my pa. My aunt took me in but I wasn't welcome. I ran as soon as I was old enough to make my own way. Headed to Denver where nobody knew me. Met Abby and we came here because she had a hankering to settle in a small town."

"I am really sorry about your pa but that has nothing to do with Nandita and her children." Sorcha turned back to look at him. "They weren't even alive then."

"It's in the blood, Sorcha. We can't help ourselves."

"Don't you mean they?" Sorcha stared at him for a few seconds. "What do you mean it's in the blood?"

"My pa was at Sand Creek."

"So what?"

"The massacre, Sorcha. Pa killed loads of Indians and not just men but mainly woman and children. That's why he drank so much. He had to forget. He used to rave about them in his dreams. The sights he saw. He couldn't ever forget."

Sorcha put her arms around him as he broke down. "He said he was cursed. His whole line was cursed and he was right. Abby died because of me. Ethan too. I can't lose anyone else."

"The Indians didn't kill Abby or Ethan. That was a freak accident, a tragedy. Nobody is to blame, least of all you. Your pa was a soldier. He had to live with his actions but you are not him. You were only a child yourself when Sand Creek happened, Brian. The same age as Jenny. Do you think Jenny would be responsible if you were to kill Nandita and her family?"

"But if Nandita knew, then she would tell the braves and they would hunt me and my children down. They'd kill you just as quick."

"You don't know that. From what I have seen, the tribe is peaceful."

"Try telling that to the Eblers."

"The Eblers were killed by dog soldiers. We don't

know if they came from the same tribe as Nandita. Indians are just like us Brian. They have good and bad people too. But the actions of a small minority shouldn't mean they all suffer." Sorcha took a deep breath. She let her arms fall to her side. He wanted to tell her to put them back. He liked the feel of her against his body. But he couldn't speak.

"Please think about your children. They are too young to be kept away from everyone. They need friends and family around them." Sorcha paused biting her cheek. "I would give anything for a real family." Sorcha's voice quivered.

He wondered if she was thinking of her sister, the one the Nun had told her about. From what she had told him, she didn't even know if she was real or a figment of the Mother Superior's twisted imagination. The pain in her voice made him feel worse.

"You have a family. Jenny, Meggie and… Me."

"Do I?"

With that, Sorcha walked away.

CHAPTER 47

He watched her leave. She was right. He had to make changes now or life would continue to be miserable. He killed a couple of minutes putting away some tools. He was trying to find the courage to make changes. He shook his head at his actions and walked purposely to the house.

"Something smells good. I've washed up." He shook his hands, trying to make her laugh but it didn't work. He let them fall to the side.

Sorcha looked a little ragged, as if the tension between them was getting to her too. Silence lingered as she dished up the dinner, handing him the meat to carve. He stared at it before looking quickly around him. They were alone. Putting the dish on the table, he quickly moved closer to her. Taking her gently in his arms, he watched her eyes open wide as his lips grazed hers. Smiling, he pulled her closer and deepened the kiss. A giggle from behind them ruined the moment.

"Pa is kissing Ma, Jenny. Look." Meggie lisped giggling.

Jenny pulled her chair out loudly. Sorcha pushed him away, the palms of her hands searing through his clothes. He wished his children were anywhere but in the house. If they had been alone, he would have taken Sorcha back in his arms and explored that kiss. Frustrated, he scowled at Meggie who immediately stopped giggling.

The next morning, Brian had to go back to Denver. Cal Sutton was buying more horses and was adamant he couldn't make the decision without Brian. He paid top dollar, and although he would have preferred to stay at the house with his wife and children, he had to go.

"Sorcha, it shouldn't be too long a trip this time."

Sorcha nodded but didn't turn around. Disappointed he looked to his children. "Are you going to give me a hug?"

"Do you have to go now, Pa? Sorcha and I wanted to discuss something with you." Jenny's eyes darted from him to Sorcha and back again.

"Can it wait?" Brian looked toward Sorcha, who seemed to be concentrating very hard on the washing up. "I really need to go now or I will miss the train."

"It'll keep." Sorcha spoke but her sad voice made his leaving even harder. "Be safe."

Brian moved to go to her but she turned back to the dishes. He stared at her back for a couple of seconds. Should he try to kiss her goodbye? He would but the children were there. He didn't want to do anything to upset them further.

SHE STOOD, wishing he would leave but not wanting him to go. The hairs on the back of her neck stood up, waiting to see if he would kiss her goodbye. Couldn't he see she was upset? Turn around and make it easier for him? *No, then he will know I love him. I can't.* The door closing caused her to jump although he hadn't slammed it. She kept her gaze focused on the dishes in front of her as the tears streamed down her cheeks. Would she ever feel like a proper wife?

"Shall I stay home today, Sorcha?" Jenny asked a while after Brian had left. Sorcha looked up from blacking the stove. She always cleaned when her mind was busy with something. "No, you go on, love. Have a good day. Don't forget to take an apple and some biscuits with you. I will make bread later so you can have a sandwich tomorrow."

"Can I take extra for Emily?"

Sorcha's heart swelled as she looked at Jenny. She was a good girl. With some more attention from her father, she would really blossom. They would all bloom. Sorcha rubbed the stove harder. Charlie Stanton should be ashamed of himself. He made enough money but Emily never had any lunch. Jenny had confided she often shared hers with the little girl, as did Miss Freeman. "Yes love, take extra."

CHAPTER 48

Jenny walked slowly off to school, leaving Meggie and Sorcha alone. Sorcha watched her stepdaughter until she disappeared over the hill. She hadn't skipped toward town as she usually did. Her pa's absence must be really affecting her.

Soon it was time for Nandita to call. She had a way of telling when Brian was away. Sorcha didn't know how her friend knew but she didn't care. She hated being alone and if Brian didn't know, then it couldn't hurt him. *You are deceitful and evil.* Sorcha pushed Mother Superior's voice aside. She wasn't under the protection of the nun anymore. Her friendship with Nandita was important to both of them. Nobody was going to take that away from her.

The day passed quite quickly. Meggie enjoyed

playing with Ama and Salali. Nandita helped Sorcha with some chores before she taught the Indian how to make white man's bread. The time passed when Jenny should have been home but there was no sign. Growing more concerned as the hours passed, Sorcha's asked Nandita to stay with Meggie while she checked on Jenny.

"No, let me go. I will find her faster."

Before Sorcha could say anything, Nandita jumped on her horse and was gone. Sorcha amused the children but they must have picked up on her emotions. They whined until Nandita returned, cradling Jenny in front of her.

"Sorry, Sorcha. I wasn't feeling well. I sat down and couldn't get back up. My legs feel funny."

Nandita and Sorcha exchanged concerned looks over Jenny's head. Feeling the little girl's forehead, she couldn't detect a fever although her skin was cold and clammy.

"Come on, love, let's get you to bed. A good sleep will do you the world of good."

"I gave Emily my lunch. I wasn't hungry. She was so happy." Jenny's glazed eyes turned in Sorcha's direction but it was as if she couldn't see her.

"Good girl. Are you hungry now? I can fix you something quick." Jenny was always starving when she came home from school.

"Maybe after I sleep." Jenny's eyes were closing as she almost fell onto the bed. "So tired."

Sorcha went to get a glass of water but Jenny was fast asleep by the time she came back. Leaving the sleeping girl, she met Nandita in the kitchen.

"You sleep near Jenny tonight. I do not like color of skin. She too white."

When once Sorcha would have laughed at Nandita's remark, she didn't today. Jenny did look too white. She bit her lip continuously wishing Brian was here. He would know what to do.

CHAPTER 49

She didn't get much sleep as Jenny thrashed about when the fever hit. She sponged her down as gently as she could. The child whimpered as if every touch was torture. *Brian come home, please come home.*

"How is she?" Nandita's voice startled Sorcha. She rubbed her neck, the pain in it a welcome distraction from the sight of her stepdaughter lying in the throes of fever.

"She's way too hot. I tried sponging her but it seems to hurt her when I touch her. What do I do now?"

Nandita reached out to touch the child's forehead. The frown on her face grew deeper, her eyes widening with fear followed by concern.

"I go now to collect some things we use to help sick

people. I wish we had the medicine man. He would know what to do."

Nandita didn't take long and soon had a brew mixed up.

"Eeew, that smells revolting."

"It tastes better than it smells. I do not know the white man name for the fruit but it will help with fever. Try it."

Sorcha hesitated. Why wasn't Brian back? What if Jenny died?

"She has a better chance if we help her fight." Nandita said gently as she stared down at the child. "You must try. She is getting worse."

Sorcha couldn't disagree. The last few hours had seen a marked deterioration. Jenny was barely conscious. When she did wake up, her speech was slurred and rambling. She took the cup and brought it to Jenny's mouth. Holding the child up slightly so she didn't choke, she dribbled some of the liquid into her mouth. Jenny gagged but didn't vomit. She laid the child back on the bed. *Dear Lord please. Make her better.*

The next three days and nights merged into each other as the two adults worked hard looking after the girls. Meggie had fallen ill the morning after Jenny had come home from school. Nandita's children seemed to have escaped. Going outside, Sorcha let the tears rain down her cheeks.

Why was God so cruel? He had answered her prayers for a family. Now he was taking them away. Just as she had let them all into her heart. They were dying and there was nothing she could do about it. Nandita was worried too. Her friend paced the floor, in between sponging the girls and feeding them the evil smelling drink.

"You must go for help. My medicine is not working. I will stay here."

"I don't want to leave them. Can you go?" Sorcha looked from the girls to Nandita and back again. She couldn't leave them now. Not when they needed her.

"No. It is not possible for me to go to white man's town. Your people will not listen to me. They may stop me from coming back. You have to go. Can you ride a horse?"

Sorcha couldn't. Yet another failure.

"Little Beaver will take you on my horse. It is safe. Sit behind him."

"But is he not in danger too?" Sorcha said as she climbed onto the horse behind the boy.

"I have to trust your people will not harm a child." The child in front of Sorcha bristled. "You must go. Now."

CHAPTER 50

Little Beaver didn't say much as they rode into town. She was grateful. She arrived at Clover Springs but was puzzled to find it was almost deserted. "Where is everyone?"

Little Beaver pulled the horse to a stop. "Go now. I go back to Nandita."

"No, wait." Sorcha didn't want to be alone.

"It is best they do not see me. I do not share Nandita's belief that they will not harm me. She does not consider me a man. I do not want to prove her wrong by fighting in your village." He looked at her for a couple of seconds as if waiting for an answer. When she didn't say anything, he turned to go.

His legs clenched into the side of his horse as he looked over his shoulder. "Your people will take you home."

Sorcha stared at the cloud of dust in his trail. Maybe he was right. She didn't know many of the Clover Springs residents but the stories Nandita had told her were sufficient to make his actions seem reasonable.

Picking up her skirt, she hurried to the store but was surprised to find it shut. She tried looking through the window but couldn't see anyone. Knocking on the door didn't work either.

She couldn't give up. Jenny and Meggie needed her. The doctor would help. She didn't know where he was but Reverend Timmons would. She ran towards the church but stopped short as she stumbled into the middle of a funeral procession.

"I'm so sorry." Sorcha apologized to a man whose foot she trod on.

The man gave her a dirty look. "Who are you? I don't recognize you. We have enough problems without strangers bringing more danger to the town."

"I came for help. I need the doctor."

The man made an ugly sound. "Doc is busy right now. With our own folk. We got us an epidemic. The whole town is sick."

Katie. Ella. Was that why the store was shut? Cold shivers of fear ran down her back. "What type of epidemic?"

"Doc says it's measles but I don't know. I ain't caught nothing and that's the way I want it to stay." He hobbled away so quickly Sorcha could have laughed if the situation wasn't so dire. Measles. Was that what the girls had?

CHAPTER 51

Staring around at the small crowd exiting the church, she tried to find a face she recognized.

"What are you doing here?" She jumped as the woman's voice came from right behind her. "You're that Irish girl, aren't you? The one Petersen married to give a new Ma to his girls."

"I'm Sorcha Petersen. I need help. Brian is away on business and his girls are sick."

"How sick?" The woman stood with her hands on her hips looking Sorcha up and down. By her expression, Sorcha saw she'd been found wanting. She didn't care. Nobody's opinion of her mattered. She had to get help for the girls.

"They have a fever and shivers. They're coughing and won't eat. Nandita thinks Jenny will die. She sent me to town to get help. I need to find the doctor." Sorcha's tone was shrill. She struggled to regain her composure. It wouldn't do to antagonize someone who could help. She looked at the woman again to see the red flush creep up her neck into her face.

"Nandita? Do you mean to say you left those Petersen girls with a…savage? Of all the…"

"Nandita isn't a savage. She's my friend. Excuse me. I need to find the doctor." Sorcha couldn't move as the woman grabbed her arm.

"They are all like that. Murder you in your bed as soon as look at ye. Is that what you want? To get rid of those poor girls?"

"What? No, of course not. Let me go. I need to get back." Sorcha pulled at her arm but the lady was stronger than she looked.

The woman didn't seem to hear her but continued ranting. "Those Petersen girls are mighty pretty. By the time you get home, there won't be a sign of them."

Sorcha swayed, seeing three of the woman in front of her. Her hate-filled face was moving in triplicate. She reached out wildly for something to hold onto as the ground moved beneath her.

"You're wrong." Sorcha blinked rapidly. The woman was wrong. Nandita was her friend, she had worked herself into the ground trying to save Brian's daughters. Her own children had been at risk too.

"Mrs. Petersen, what is wrong with the girls?" Sorcha heard a new voice questioning her but she couldn't focus to respond. A stinging clap across the cheek got her attention. "Come on, out with it, girl. What's happened to Jenny and Meggie?"

"They are sick, really sick. I think they may have measles."

"Dear God. Where is Mr. Petersen? Is he sick too?"

Sorcha shook her head so hard it made her dizzier. "No, well, I don't think so. He went away. To Denver." Sorcha turned away. "I have to go get the doctor. The girls need me."

"No chance of the doctor going with you. Too many patients need him here in town."

Sorcha moved her hand over her stomach afraid she would empty it right there in front of the ladies. "Please. Someone has to come. The girls could die. I can't let that happen." Sorcha held out her hand to the older woman. "Please help me. Nandita's medicine isn't working. I don't know what to do." Sorcha stood wringing her hands together.

"See, I told you. Stupid girl has let injuns loose on those lovely girls. They'll be ruined."

"They'll be dead unless I get them help." Sorcha stood straighter, ignoring the bad tempered woman who still had a hold on her arm. Nobody was going to stop her getting help for her girls. "You may consider

Nandita a savage but at least she helped me. Which is more than can be said for either of you."

Sorcha pulled away and turned on her heel so fast it caught in her skirt. She would have fallen head first if the nicer woman hadn't made a grab for her.

"You have spirit. Have you a wagon?"

"No Little... I got a ride here."

"Go to Frank and get him to hitch up a wagon. I am too old to go to your home by horseback. I need some supplies. Meet me at the store. Hurry."

"The store is shut."

"Not for me. Katie will let me in."

Realization dawned on Sorcha. "Are you Mrs. Grey?"

The woman nodded before saying. "Don't stand there gawping at me, girl. Go get the wagon."

"Yes, ma'am." Gathering her skirts, Sorcha ran in the direction of Frank's stables. She knew all about Mrs. Grey from Mary's letters. She saved Katie, maybe she can save the girls too. *Thank you Lord.*

CHAPTER 52

Sorcha pulled up the wagon outside the store. She'd had a job convincing Frank not to come with her. She didn't want to expose him to whatever illness was in her home. He seemed concerned Nandita was at the house. She didn't think he saw the Indian as a threat but seemed worried about her. She didn't have time to dwell on that now.

She didn't go into the store for fear of infecting Katie or baby Ella but sat counting backwards in Irish. Just as Granny had told her to do when her troubles threatened to overcome her. She wished Granny was here now. She moved over as Mrs. Grey insisted on driving back to the house. The old woman rode the wagon hard with Sorcha holding onto the sides for dear life. There wasn't time for conversation.

They had barely stopped when Mrs. Grey started

issuing orders. "Get some hot water going and plenty of clean rags. Tell that boy to go get as many berries as he can. Nandita, boil up some of that brew you use for fevers. Now where are the girls?"

Sorcha didn't answer. She was too busy staring after Nandita and Little Beaver who had jumped to do Mrs. Grey's bidding. "The girls, Mrs. Petersen. Are you sure you are not sick too? You seem to be ailing."

Sorcha pulled herself together. She wasn't going to fall apart on the girls now. She showed Mrs. Grey into her bedroom where the two girls were sharing a bed. She studied the woman's face as she examined the girls.

"Is it measles? Are you not afraid?"

"You can't get it again. I must have had it as a child as I didn't catch it off our soldiers. We need to separate these girls."

"Meggie cries if she can't see Jenny." Sorcha protested.

"Do you want her dead or upset?"

Sorcha then knew what the phrase *your blood ran cold* meant. Dead. She couldn't lose either of the girls.

"Listen, child. Meggie isn't as ill as Jenny. She has a very good chance of survival but only if we separate them." For some reason, Mrs. Grey being nice was more worrying than her issuing orders. Sorcha dreaded what was to come. The older woman paused for a moment staring down at Jenny. She pushed the hair back from her eyes.

"Jenny, well frankly, you should prepare yourself for the worst. She is a very sick little girl."

No. YOU can't have her too. You took Granny and Luke. Everyone who loved me. Sorcha railed at God before turning on Mrs. Grey.

"I am not losing her, Mrs. Grey. God just gave me a family and I'm darn well not going to hand it back to him on a plate." Sorcha stood still. Would Mrs. Grey leave? She had just sworn. Typical of her to let her tongue run away with her. Instead of scolding her, the woman smiled.

"Good girl. That's the spirit we need. Have you had measles?"

Sorcha shrugged. "I guess so. I don't know."

"No use worrying about that now. We'll know soon enough. You tell me if you feel ill. You hear?"

"Yes, ma'am."

"You nurse Meggie in the girls' room. I will tend to Jenny in here."

"Please let me tend Jenny." Sorcha begged.

"You, girl, need some rest. You are exhausted. As is Nandita. Go to bed and you can take over in the morning."

"I won't sleep." Sorcha protested despite every bone in her body screaming with tiredness.

"Oh, but you will. Hasn't your friend Mary told you? I don't expect any disobedience. I just won't tolerate it."

Sorcha thought she saw a twinkle in the other woman's eye but it was gone as quick as it came. She pushed herself to her feet. Making up a pallet on the floor of the girls room, she returned to take Meggie. "Can't I just sleep beside her?"

"And risk her fever increasing? Not to mention the risk of infecting you. Absolutely not. Do as you are told."

Instinctively Sorcha moved to argue but Mrs. Grey spoke over her. "Save your strength to fight the disease not my orders."

Sorcha fought the urge to salute. She must be crazy. She moved Meggie quickly before coming back into the room to give Jenny a kiss. Stumbling out of the room, her vision blurred with tears. Mrs. Grey caught her arm. "Sorcha, I will do my best. Pray for God's mercy, dear."

Sorcha didn't trust her voice to work. She squeezed the other woman's arm gratefully before moving out of the room. She checked on Nandita and her children but they were all fast asleep.

Taking a large glass of water, she went back to Meggie. The child was restless, tossing and turning on the pallet. Sorcha put her hand on the little one's forehead. It felt cooler than before. She sponged her down again with the concoction Nandita had boiled first then cooled. She barely noticed the smell as she prayed for God's mercy.

Dear Father above, save my children. Don't let their deaths be the price I pay for my foolishness. Brian was right. I shouldn't have insisted on taking Jenny to school. She'd be happy and healthy now if only I had listened. Sorcha remained on her knees until Mrs. Grey came into the room.

"Get into bed with you. This isn't the time to be making yourself ill. I have enough to do without nursing you as well."

"It's my fault the girls are sick. I took them to school. Their pa didn't want them in town."

"Children belong in school. You weren't to know there were measles around. Nobody was." Mrs. Grey examined Meggie. She smoothed down the sheet covering the little girl before turning her attention back to Sorcha. "Don't know what it is about you Catholics. You are always looking for something to feel guilty about."

Sorcha frowned. Why was Mrs. Grey not telling her how worthless she was? Maybe she needed to speak plainly. "If they stayed here, they wouldn't have gotten sick."

"God is all powerful. He's the one who makes the

decisions over who gets what, who dies, who lives. The sooner you accept that, the better. Make life easier for all of us, especially these girls. They've been through enough."

Sorcha couldn't reply. Mrs. Grey left taking the lamp with her. Sorcha lay in the darkness. Was Mrs. Grey right? Would God have sent this epidemic to their little house anyway? She tossed and turned, images of the girls mixed with Mother Superior and Brian. She sat up in a cold sweat. When would he be home? What was he going to do when he found out she had put their girls at risk?

CHAPTER 53

Bright light hit her eyeballs. Pain seared through her head. She was so tired. The last two days had been a continuous round of nursing and cleaning. She did everything Mrs. Grey asked. Nandita worked just as hard but they couldn't see a difference in the girls. Mrs. Grey had insisted Sorcha rest. She had gone to bed, protesting she didn't need sleep and here she was trying not to wake up.

She tried to close her eyes but small fingers prevented her. "Sorra, wake up. Meggie hungry."

Sorcha twisted trying to find the darkness. She didn't want to face the world today. She tried to clench her eyes shut.

"Sorra." The tone was more insistent as she shook her. *Meggie!*

Sorcha jumped up from the pallet bed, grabbing

Meggie into a big cuddle. "Meggie, what are you doing out of bed?" Her forehead was cool to the touch.

"Sorra, Meggie hungry." As if to emphasize the point, the child pointed to her belly. Squealing with laughter, Sorcha swung Meggie around. She was fine. She had survived.

"Come on, love. Let's go find you something to eat." She carried the child out to the kitchen where Nandita was cooking. "She's better. The fever has broken."

Nandita's smile reached her eyes for the first time since the girls had gotten sick.

"Where's Jenny?" Meggie asked her finger curling into her mouth.

Sorcha and Nandita exchanged looks before Sorcha pulled Meggie onto her lap. "Jenny is still sick, love. You sit down here and let Nandita give you breakfast. I will go see how Jenny is."

"Meggie come too." The child's grip tightened uncomfortably around her neck. Sorcha knew she couldn't risk infecting the toddler again. She peeled the little arms from her all the time saying softy. "You need to be a big girl now, Meggie, and help Sorcha. Sit down and eat. I will be back in a minute."

At the mutinous expression on the child's face, Nandita spoke. "Mrs. Grey is looking after Jenny."

They would have laughed at the speed Meggie took

her chair and held up her spoon had they not been so worried about her sister.

CHAPTER 54

Sorcha knocked on the door of her bedroom. Hearing no response, she pushed it open. Mrs. Grey was slumped over in the chair. The poor lady had fallen asleep. Sorcha took a blanket and put it over her. Turning to Jenny, she put a hand to her mouth at the sight before her. The girl was covered in spots. Her face glistened with sweat. Taking a seat on the other side of the bed, Sorcha bathed her with the evil smelling liquid.

"Ma, is that you?" The child's weak whisper pierced Sorcha's heart.

"It's Sorcha, love."

"Am I going to die?" Jenny whispered. "I don't want to. I won't go to heaven. I've been too nasty."

Sorcha put the cloth down and pulled the child to

her. "You are not going to die. I won't let you." Jenny's eyes closed over. "Fight, Jenny. I love you, sweetheart."

Jenny's eyes flickered open.

"I'm scared. Will you sing to me?"

Sorcha swallowed but nothing shifted the lump in her throat. "I don't think I can, love."

"Please, Sorcha."

Sorcha hummed a couple of verses for Jenny as she took back up the cloth and sponged the child all over. She watched the little girl's face relax slightly as sleep took over. *I will not let you die. I just won't. I don't care what anyone else says.*

Mrs. Grey stirred in her chair. "Sorcha, how is she?"

"She's burning up."

"Did she wake up? She was muttering a lot last night but I couldn't make out what she was trying to say."

Sorcha wiped Jenny's face again with the cloth, the tears in her eyes blurring her vision. "She told me she's scared of dying. She thinks she won't go to …" Sorcha put her head on the bed beside Jenny's hand and sobbed her heart out. She loved the child so much. She couldn't lose her now.

Standing, Mrs. Grey checked Jenny before putting a hand on Sorcha's shoulders.

"Come on. Pull yourself together. We have to bathe

her. Bring the tub in here. We have to try to get that fever down."

Sorcha wiped her eyes, gave Jenny a quick kiss and moved toward the door. Mrs. Grey looked pale and anxious.

"Mrs. Grey, you should rest."

"Plenty of time for that when this is over."

Sorcha gripped the door handle. Had she misheard? Surely Mrs. Grey hadn't given up.

"Don't stand there gawping. I'm not done yet. Get that tub and ask Nandita to come in here."

Sorcha moved but then turned back to the old lady. "Meggie is much better. She is eating breakfast." The transformation in Mrs. Grey's face was incredible. Her soft expression hinted at the beauty she must have been in her youth. Then the mask descended once more.

"Don't let her eat too much. Her system is still weak. Last thing we need is her vomiting everywhere."

Sorcha reeled. She didn't know what to make of this woman. One minute she had the heart of an angel, the next she was as fierce as a cornered bear. *Thank God she is on our side.*

"Sorra, is Jenny coming to eat breakfast too?" Meggie's voice intruded on her thoughts.

She looked at her little girl, the thumb back in her

mouth as she waited for an answer. "No, love. Mrs. Grey wants Jenny to have a bath."

"Meggie no want a bath."

Sorcha took the child up into her arms and gave her a big cuddle. "You don't need a bath, love. Not today. Little Beaver will take you girls outside to play. Nandita and I are going to help give Jenny a bath."

A quick glance at Nandita was enough to tell the Indian girl the situation was serious. Meggie didn't need to see or hear what would transpire over the next few hours.

"Meggie, why don't you see if you can find flowers for Jenny? She can see them when she wakes up."

Sorcha could hear the tremor in Nandita's voice. Meggie's clap of approval at the Indian's suggestion made her wish she was an innocent child too, completely unaware of the hardships life had to offer.

CHAPTER 55

Brian walked slowly with the horse following behind. Typical, he had to go lame just a couple of miles from the house. He was looking forward to seeing his girls again. Jenny, Meggie and Sorcha. Sorcha. He hadn't stopped thinking about her when he was away. She wasn't fragile or delicate as he had first thought. She had shown fire and spirit not to mention strength of character.

He knew of her friendship with Nandita. While not thrilled his young wife had deceived him, Frank had made him see that preventing her from having company was wrong. Nandita was a nice girl. *For an Indian.*

Coming over the rise, he could see the house in the distance. Tempting as it was to walk faster, he couldn't do that to Jackson. The poor animal had been a faithful servant. With a little rest and a couple of healing hot compresses, his leg should be fine but only if he didn't push him.

Looking at the house, his stomach pitched. Something was wrong. He couldn't see any movement and there was a strange wagon parked outside. A high pitched scream carried in the wind.

Dropping his bags, he ran faster than he ever did before. Jenny. His little girl was in trouble. Her screams made him run even faster. He burst into the house to find three women drowning the child in water. He pulled the Indian away first before turning his full fury on his wife.

"What are you doing?"

"Mr. Petersen, please control yourself. You are scaring Jenny."

Jenny wasn't screaming anymore but moaning. It took a few minutes for his brain to account for her glazed eyes and mottled skin.

"Brian, Jenny has measles. We need to get her temperature down. We tried everything else but this is our last chance." Sorcha pulled at his arm. He looked toward her but couldn't take in what she was saying. Measles. How did his daughter have measles?

"Move out of my way. You will kill her." He pushed Sorcha away to his side and then scooped Jenny from the water. His little girl clung to him. "Pa." That one word told him he was doing the right thing. He cuddled her shivering body closer.

"Lay her on the bed, Mr. Petersen. We need to get her dry before she gets too chilled." Jenny's teeth were chattering so hard, the vibrations moved up his arms. Mrs. Grey led the way to his bedroom, laying some towels on the bed before looking at him pointedly. "Let us try to save your child."

He looked from the old woman to his daughter and back again. Something on her face told him to do as he was bid. He laid Jenny gently on the bed covering her quickly with a towel.

"I will call you in as soon as she is decent."

The dismissal was pointed and didn't brook an argument. Shoulders slumping as the fight left him, he walked back into the main room. Nandita and his wife were emptying the tub. He stared at them for a few minutes, taking in the fear in Nandita's eyes and the fact his wife wouldn't look at him.

"Nandita, please leave us."

Nandita looked to Sorcha, who nodded slightly. With one last glance at him, she obeyed his request. He clenched and unclenched his hands trying to calm his temper.

"Sorcha, what were you doing to Jenny? I heard her screaming."

"She didn't want to get into the bath. The water was very cold. But it was the only way, I swear to you."

He walked slowly around the tub not wanting to scare her.

"I know that now." He put his hand on her arm, causing her to wince. "Did I hurt you?" A vision of him pushing her aside hit him.

"Tis nothing more than I deserve."

At his wife's whisper, he sat on the nearest chair and buried his head in his hands. *Dear Lord, don't punish me again. Don't take Jenny away from me. Please.*

"MR. PETERSEN, WAKE UP." Brian woke with a start to face Mrs. Grey. He shot out of the chair.

"Jenny."

"Jenny is fine, thanks in no small part to your wife and her Indian friend. She is sleeping now. The fever has broken. Your little girl will be soon back at school where she belongs."

Brian rubbed the sleep from his eyes. "School? No, Mrs. Grey you must be mistaken. Jenny doesn't attend school."

"I am not often wrong, Mr. Petersen. Now you can take that look off your face. Your child needs to attend school, not just for an education, but also for her social development. Before you go blaming school for your child being sick, the majority of people who fell ill in town weren't children. They say some ill people came in by train some days ago." Mrs. Grey made a point of dusting down her skirts, allowing him some thinking time. "Your wife is an educated lady. Exactly the type of woman Clover Springs needs."

My wife is amazing. She also defied you and went against your wishes. Brian dismissed the voice. He'd been wrong. He couldn't protect Jenny by keeping her here on the homestead. Any one of his customers could have carried measles with them.

God hadn't taken his Jenny but he had sent him a wonderful gift. Now if he could only find a way to tell his wife he loved her.

CHAPTER 56

"You look sad, my friend. Jenny, she is all right now. I think she go back to school?"

"Yes, Jenny is great. You wouldn't know she's been sick."

"And you? You are sick in here, yes?" Nandita pointed at her heart.

Sorcha looked into the distance. She didn't want to have this discussion.

"I am fine."

"Really?" Nandita held her head to one side as she always did when thinking. "You seem to get smaller every time I see you. Are you not eating?"

"Stop fussing." Sorcha picked at her skirt. "I eat enough."

"So why you look so miserable? You sing sad songs too. Make everyone cry."

"Do I?"

Nandita just stared back at her.

"That's the Irish in me. All our songs speak of going home."

"Home? This is your home now, no?"

"Yes."

"But it is not enough. You want to make a home with your husband. Maybe when you have a baby?"

"Nandita." Sorcha's cheeks flamed. "Don't."

"I do not understand you white women. You don't speak about babies or what happens between a husband and wife. Why?"

"It's private, I guess." Sorcha's burning cheeks and the shivers going up and down her spine made it impossible for her to look at Nandita. *Never mind, sit still, and ladylike.*

"Don't you want a baby? I know you love the girls but one of your own. It's different, yes?"

"Yes." Sorcha whispered. Not because she thought the girls would hear her. They were too far away. She was afraid to put her thoughts into words for fear they would sound stupid. "I would like a real marriage."

"You mean you would like your husband to share your blanket."

Sorcha giggled. "Yes, my dear blunt friend. I would like that."

"Why not ask him?"

Sorcha shook her head violently. "I can't do that. It would be too forward."

"You are married. You say words in front of your medicine man. It is not right he sleep in the barn. He cannot give you a baby with him out there."

"Stop, please."

"Do you not want him as your husband? He seems like a kind man."

"How can you of all people say that? He's never been nice to you."

"I see how he is with the horses and other sick animals. A man who is gentle and caring. He has many sorrows in his heart."

"The loss of his wife and his son."

"Yes, they are recent sorrows but he has much more. From when he was a child. I look in his eyes and I see much sadness." Nandita took Sorcha's hand, rubbing it gently. "I see much pain in your eyes too, my friend. You spend too much time thinking of the past. You must live for the future. What has gone on before cannot be changed. But what happens tomorrow. That is up to you."

Sorcha took her hand back. She stared into the distance.

"You care deeply for him, don't you?"

Sorcha couldn't answer, her throat closing as the emotions welled up inside her.

"Show him how you feel. Together you can heal the pain."

"I don't know how." Sorcha's temper rose with her voice. "I try to cook him the food he likes, wash his clothes, sew his socks but nothing gets his attention." Surprised, she stopped as Nandita laughed loudly.

"Sew his socks. I mean you should get his attention as a lover not as his mother. You need to touch him."

"I couldn't. Could I?" Sorcha closed her eyes, barely peeping at Nandita from under her lashes. "How?"

"It is very easy." Nandita's eyes sparkled with mischief. "Stand very near when you are speaking to him. Touch him. On the arm or leg – you can pretend it is an accident. Let your hair free. I do not understand why white women always bunch their hair up on top of their heads. It make them look like an upside down bush."

Sorcha giggled. Nandita did too, as she pulled her long dark hair into a funny shaped bun. "See, I look like I am wearing a bush."

"Did you use these tricks on your hus… I am so sorry, Nandita." Sorcha's stomach twisted at the hurt and pain in her friend's face. She was so stupid.

"It is ok. No. With Sleeping Bear, I did not wish to

use any tricks. He needed no help taking what he thought was his." A fierce glow lit up her brown eyes. Sorcha could have bitten through her own tongue. Why did she mention him? She held her hand out to her friend wanting to take away those horrible memories.

"Do your hands always look like that after you wash clothes?"

Sorcha rubbed self-consciously at her hands, although she knew this was Nandita's way of changing the subject.

"They look painful."

"Granny told me it was the soap but sure what choice do I have? You can't wash clothes with just water."

Nandita walked over to her things. Bending down, she retrieved a small bowl.

"Try rubbing this on them. It won't hurt and it may help a little. I too have same problem." Nandita gave her the bowl. "I made some this morning. It will keep for a few days. If it helps, I will show you how to make it."

"Thank you." Sorcha eyed her friend. "Have you heard any more about Sleeping Bear?"

Nandita eyes darkened. "He is recovering from his injuries. They say he will be well enough to travel in a few days. He will come for us soon."

"Oh, Nandita. Do you have to go with him? Can you not stay here?"

"I don't think your husband would like that."

"Well, not here, but with the other Indians? Would they not take you in?"

"Some of them would, but the majority are too worried about their own families. There isn't enough food to go around. They have too many women and children and not enough men. They know they will soon be forced to live on the reservation in Montana. They have tried running once but now they have accepted defeat."

"But they can't expect you to live with a man who beats you? Next time he might kill you."

"He will. He has said so." Nandita's brown eyes widened. Before Sorcha could ask why, he spoke.

"Who will kill you?"

"Brian, I'm sorry. I know you said Nandita was not to come again." Sorcha stopped speaking.

"Who?"

"My husband, Sleeping Bear. He…he hates me and wants me dead."

"Why doesn't your family protect you?"

"I have no family. My father was killed years ago. The tribe let my mother and me stay with them. When I left Sleeping Bear, I left the tribe too."

"She can't go back to him, Brian, please tell her she

doesn't have to." Sorcha went to put a hand on her husband's arm but at the last second, let it fall away.

He looked at her hand first, before his eyes travelled up to meet hers. She saw what she thought was regret in his face. But his tone was hard. "We cannot get involved in Indian business, Sorcha. You know that."

"It's not Indian business. She's my friend. She saved your child." She didn't stamp her foot but she wanted to.

"Sorcha, your husband speaks true. Sleeping Bear is a bad enemy. The sprits will protect me. Maybe it is my time to join my parents."

"No. I don't believe that. You are young. Frank will help you. I know he will." Sorcha put her hand to her mouth. She had promised herself to say nothing of the visits that took place between Frank and her friend. Nandita didn't speak of them and neither had Frank. But she had seen the way he looked at the Indian girl. A look of love that was returned every time Nandita saw him but thought nobody else was watching.

"Leave Frank out of this."

"But Nandita…"

"Sorcha, I said no. It is too much risk to everyone."

CHAPTER 57

Brian stood watching silently. The girl was very brave. Frank too. He'd suspected his friend had more personal feelings than he had let on. Sorcha's comments had confirmed the suspicions. They, Nandita and Frank, had each suffered enough already. He should try to help them. Frank was his friend. Nandita had tried her best to save Jenny. Mrs. Grey had given the Indian girl the highest praise.

"Nandita, can you take me to see Chief Running Buffalo?"

"The chief? But why?"

"If you could provide for yourself and your children, would he give you shelter?"

"Well yes, but I have no way to do that. My beadwork is good but not good enough to sell."

"You can make those teas you made when my girls

were sick. I heard you tell Sorcha you could help her hands."

* * *

How long had he been listening? *Oh, please don't let him have heard Nandita telling her how to seduce him.* Sorcha concentrated hard on not giving in to the impulse to run as far away from him as possible. Instead she listened.

"Do you think enough people would buy them?" The hope in Nandita's voice brought tears to Sorcha's eyes. Angrily, she brushed them away. Her friend wasn't crying and she wasn't about to start now.

"I do not need much, but the children? They are always hungry."

"Sorcha, please pack up some food." Sorcha's heart missed a beat when he called her name. "Nandita, you and the children are welcome to stay here tonight. Tomorrow, we will go see Chief Running Buffalo."

"You are going to the Indian camp? I thought well… that is…" Sorcha closed her mouth at the determined look he gave her.

"It is time to finish this. Nandita is right. We cannot live in the past. I was wrong." Brian reached out a hand as if to caress her face. But he let it fall short. "Wrong about a lot of things. We will talk once Nandita is settled."

Sorcha hugged Nandita close before leaving her and Brian to talk. She walked back to the house alone. What did his last comment mean? Was he going to send her back to Boston? He didn't mean for her to stay. Did he?

Much as she wanted Nandita to be safe, and the children of course, she wanted Brian to explain right now what he meant. Briefly, she considered asking him but soon realized that was selfish. Her friend needed their help.

"I am going with you." Sorcha said, surprising everyone as she turned back to where they were standing, not least herself. "Mary will take the girls. I have to see Nandita settled for myself."

Brian opened his mouth but closed it again quickly at a look from Nandita.

"It is right you both come. There is much to be settled."

Sorcha got the feeling Nandita was talking about more than just her situation but she wasn't getting into that now. There wasn't time. She had to pack up her things as well as the girls.

The next morning, she hurried to complete her chores grateful for Nandita's help. Brian was in the barn with Frank, who had agreed to look after the horses in their absence.

Sorcha hurried out to the barn to ask her husband something. The two men were arguing but quieted down as soon as they saw her.

"What's wrong?"

"Nothing, Mrs. Petersen. Your husband was just giving me orders. You'd think I didn't know one end of the horse from another."

Sorcha looked to Brian for an explanation but there was none forthcoming. His stony expression warned her to leave it. Turning about on her heel, she marched back to the house.

Surely he wasn't discussing me with Frank? Was he?

CHAPTER 58

They headed to the Sullivan ranch shortly after midday. The girls were excited to be spending a few nights with Ben, so they didn't create too much of a fuss when they found out they weren't going to see their Indian friends.

On arrival, they found Mary shelling peas. She was delighted to take the girls for a spell but refused to let the adults leave on an empty stomach. Davy took Brian out to see some of his foals while Nandita helped Mrs. H prepare lunch. Mrs. H had been baking, so they ate their fill of delicious pastries, followed by cakes.

"Thank you for taking the girls. You will look after them should something happen?"

"Sorcha Matthews, sorry, Petersen. You will never

change. You are always so theatrical. What on earth could happen?"

"Nandita's husband doesn't like whites." Sorcha regretted the harshness of her words as her friend paled. "Sorry, Mary, I didn't mean to frighten you. It's been an eventful day. We are not going to meet Sleeping Bear, or at least, I hope we don't. Brian wishes to speak to the chief."

"Be careful. Come home soon. The girls will be here waiting for their ma and pa."

When they were leaving the ranch, Jenny ran back out after saying goodbye. She came up to Sorcha and threw her arms around her. "Be careful and come back, Ma."

Sorcha hugged the girl tightly. "I will, love, I will. Be good now and look after Meggie."

Jenny gave her another hug before running back to Mary. Davy and Ben had offered to ride with them some of the way. With one last glance at her girls, she turned to look at her husband. He smiled but his eyes were wary. Disappointed he didn't comment on Jenny calling her Ma, she turned to face the road ahead. It wasn't time to dwell on her marriage. She had to help her friend first.

CHAPTER 59

"I was waiting for you to come." The chief sat down on crossed legs and invited them to take a seat with him.

"Waiting?"

"The medicine man said to expect a visitor. He would settle the ghosts of the past. Is that why you are here, Mr. Petersen."

Brian nodded then shook his head. "No, Chief Running Buffalo, well maybe. Ah, I don't know why I am here really. The girl, Nandita. She saved my little girls. They had the fever real bad. Doc said they were going to die. Nandita looked after them. They lived. I owe her."

"No. She repaid her debt. Now you are both free."

"Debt. Nandita had no debt to pay. I had never met

her before…that first time I threw her off my property."

"No, you did not meet Nandita but does she not remind you of anyone?"

Brian didn't answer. Something in the chief's eyes made him stop.

"It was a time of great sadness for you. Your father—"

"Please don't talk about him." Brian crossed his arms across his chest, his face a stony mask. "I know all about what he did and for that I am sorry. I was only a child."

The chief fell silent, staring at Brian. The hairs on the back of his neck stood up. He had to fight the urge to jump up and run.

"Your father was a good man. A brave man."

Brian spat out the water he had just drunk. "My father. You are joking."

"Joking? What is this joking?" The chief looked so puzzled, Brian knew he was genuine.

"My father was a murderer."

"Ah, many white men believe men who kill in wars are guilty of murder. I do not understand this. To kill a man in battle is not the same as killing a woman or a child."

Brian didn't move but the sweat trickled down his back. He glanced at Sorcha and then toward the exit.

Could he get her out of the teepee if trouble erupted? Was this Indian trying to tell him something?

"Listen, Chief. I don't mean to be rude but I am not here about my father. Nandita needs help."

"The actions of your father brings you here, no?"

"Yes, no, oh heck, I don't exactly know why I am here. Nandita is my wife's friend. She seems like a nice girl and a good ma to those children. She deserves a man who doesn't beat her. I heard her tell Sorcha this Sleeping Bear will kill her." The chief didn't move. "How could you stand back and let a man kill a woman?"

"Like your father did?"

Brian's anger deflated as his shoulders fell to his chest. He couldn't look up, he didn't want Sorcha to see his shame. His pa. Why did it always come back to him?

"I am not my pa." He was mumbling but his voice refused to come out stronger. "I am very sorry for what he did to your people."

The Chief moved to touch Brian but he sprang back, not before he saw puzzlement, followed by understanding in the old man's eyes. He buried his face in his hands.

"There is much you do not understand, young man. Your father helped my people as much as it was possible for any soldier."

Brian took his face out of his hands. "What?"

"You do not know the full story but only the parts you wanted to believe. Your pa was a brave man, but he could not live with the price he paid for his bravery." The chief paused and complete silence descended on the group. It seemed like everyone held their breath. The old man was staring at Brian but not seeing him. Brian risked a glance behind him but was faced with only the hide of the tent.

"I can still see him there surrounded by the bodies of my people. My wife, my children."

CHAPTER 60

Sorcha bit her tongue to try to stop the tears from falling. The hurt on the old man's face was too much. Brian put his head back in his hands. Sorcha wanted to go to him, to comfort him, but the touch of Nandita's hand on her arm stopped her.

"I am sorry, so very sorry."

Sorcha cried as her husband begged for forgiveness. Again she moved but Nandita's firm touch sent her a message saying don't.

"Mr. Petersen. Your pa was at Sand Creek, but he didn't murder my people. He led some of the women to safety, including Nandita's mother, my favorite sister. He tried to stop the slaughter but the other men obeyed the army chief."

"But why was he broken"

"His spirit died that day. We saw things no man

should ever see. Your pa, he had a kind heart. Just like you. He cried as he carried the children to the burial grounds."

"But the army discharged him on dishonorable grounds."

Sorcha heard her husband's unspoken questions. After all this time, he couldn't believe his father had been a hero.

The chief stared at Brian for a couple of minutes while he seemed to compose his thoughts. Maybe he was looking for the right words in English. Sorcha wondered where he had learned such good use of their language. Not that it mattered. Noting mattered now but her husband getting his life back.

"He refused to go back with the other soldiers. He wrote letters to the great father in the white house. He didn't go back home for some time afterwards."

"Where did he go?"

"He stayed with us at first before he moved up into the mountains. With my sister."

The chief stopped talking and looked Brian squarely in the face. The air was charged. Sorcha suddenly saw what the chief had been hinting at. She looked from her husband to Nandita and back again. The resemblance was clearer now. How would Brian react? She watched her husband's face as the truth finally dawned on him. Shock drained all color from his face as he stared at Nandita.

The Chief spoke again, breaking the silence. "It was not safe for him here. He was a missing soldier and his army was looking for him. He was white and our people had reasons to hate the white man. I didn't know if I could protect them." The chief held Brian's arm now, as if trying to make him understand he hadn't just let his father leave. "There were many brutal attacks after Sand Creek. The dog soldiers were angry. They did many horrible things. The white men fought back. Many, many people on both sides were killed. Good people as well as bad. Love grew between my sister and your father but even it was not enough to save him."

"Why didn't he tell us?"

"He couldn't tell anyone. When he visited us later that year, he had been drinking a lot. He drank to drown out the images of that day. The men who attacked us weren't just soldiers. Some were people your father had known for years. Hans was supposed to be fighting against slavery."

The chief motioned to Nandita to get him a drink. All his talking had reduced his voice to a whisper. Sorcha edged closer toward Brian but couldn't move to his side. The chief met her eyes and sent her a plea for space.

After taking a large drink, he continued. "Hans was a good man. He couldn't believe that the men he called friends would do such things. He was crazed with grief. It changed him."

"I'd say. My pa never raised his hand in anger. He used the cane if we needed a hiding. But when he came home, he was different. He hit Ma."

Sorcha saw Brian swallow hard and wipe his arm across his eyes. But he wasn't ready to give up.

"The pa who went to war would never have touched the woman he loved. But he didn't love her anymore, did he? Not if he had taken up with a… another woman. Pa should have died that day. It would've been better for everyone." Brian went to move away from the chief but the Indian held him in a vice grip.

"Not everyone." His voice was no longer a whisper but a growl. "He saved many of our people. Not just after the massacre but by telling people what really happened. What the dog soldiers did to the white settlers was wrong. The army didn't kill the men who did that. Not then, and not when Yellow Hair killed Chief Black Kettle some years later. Your father gave us a voice when nobody else was listening."

CHAPTER 61

Silence descended once more. Sorcha risked a quick look at Nandita but she was staring at her chief. Had she known all along, or was the news a surprise to her too? Brian was looking at the ground. His sudden anger surprised all of them.

"So why did you kill him? When we got the body back, anyone could see it was Indians that killed him."

"Again, you believe that which you want to." The Chief chided Brian with a look. Sorcha saw it hit its mark as her husband's face flushed. "Your father died by his own hand. He came to our village asking us to kill him. I spoke to him. I tried to thank him for saving my sister but he would not listen to me. He would not listen to my sister either. He never knew about Nandita. He was filled with anger and hate."

"See? He hated the Indians." Brian's smug reaction showed he wasn't listening.

Chief Running Buffalo appeared to run out of patience. "No, he hated himself." His angry tone brooked no argument. "He hated what his friends did that day. It was wrong and he knew it. They weren't warriors but old or sick men, women and children." The chief settled back on his crossed legs and took a drink of water. His sad voice continued the story.

"Hans risked all. He stood against his friends. The army didn't believe him. They took everything. His job, his family and his soul."

Brian gulped loudly, sending shivers down Sorcha's back. Every nerve in her body willed her to go to him. To give him comfort, but he had to find out how the story ended. He wouldn't be free until he knew everything.

"So how did he die?" Brian asked in a quivering voice.

"He fell, and the knife he was holding went into his chest. He died very quickly. We couldn't bring him back to your home. The soldiers would have captured us." The Chief looked at Brian squarely in the eyes. "We did not desert the man who tried to save us. We did the best we could. It was not enough."

Sorcha pulled out of Nandita's restraint and ran to her husband. Putting her arms around him, she drew him back against her body as the sobs wracked his. Tears flowed as he mourned the loss of his pa and the guilt for believing all the cruel rumors that had followed their family.

Sorcha held Brian close until his body stopped shaking.

"If my pa wasn't evil, why did the Lord take Abby and Ethan in revenge?"

"I do not understand why the white man believes in a powerful being bent on revenge. Your wife and son died but it was not to pay a debt due by your father." The old man's eyes seemed to pierce through Brian. Sorcha prayed her husband was listening.

"We do not know why the great spirits act the way they do. We just have to accept that they know best. Losing your wife and son was a tragedy, but you must let them go now. Their spirits cannot rest in peace."

"I don't know how."

"Honor your wife and child. Do something in their memory. Stop living in the past and work on creating the best future you can. God has already given you many gifts." The chief took Sorcha's hand. "Thank you for looking after Nandita and her children. You are young but you have an old heart."

CHAPTER 62

The Indians withdrew quietly leaving Sorcha and Brian alone. They didn't speak but held each other close. Nandita came back some time later with food and fuel for the fire.

"Chief Running Buffalo asks you to stay the night. It is late and you are tired. You can leave tomorrow."

"No, we will go home now." Brian went to stand but Sorcha pulled on his arm.

"Thank you, Nandita. My sister. I have always wanted a sister. Please tell Chief Running Buffalo we are very grateful for his hospitality. Tomorrow we would ask for more of his time."

Nandita's eyebrows rose but before she could ask anything, Sorcha stole a quick look at Brian. Then she took her friend's hand. "Nandita, Brian came here to help you. We will not leave until you and your children, his family, are safe."

Tears filled Nandita's eyes matched by those in Sorcha's. They hugged silently before the Indian girl left. Leaving her alone with Brian.

She sat down beside the fire heating up the food Nandita had brought in. He didn't say a word the whole time she worked. She handed him a plate and only then did he seem to realize she was present.

"I'm not hungry, but thank you." He tried to smile but it didn't reach his eyes.

"You must eat. Today was hard but you have to help Nandita tomorrow. You gave your word."

Brian picked up the plate. There wasn't any cutlery so he ate using his hands. He didn't seem to taste anything but cleared the plate very quickly.

"Thank you for being here today, Sorcha." He looked at her closely. "Are you happy?"

"I'm grand." Sorcha said, but she couldn't look at him.

"The chief was right. I am blind to the gifts I have been given. I was wrong to try to ignore my feelings for you."

She felt him wipe his hands on his pants before turning to brush the side of her face. He gently forced her to look at him.

"You, on the other hand, have been caring and loving since the day you stepped off the train. I've behaved like a cantankerous old mule. Can you ever forgive me?"

Sorcha couldn't answer. She was caught in his gaze. She let him pull her closer until he was close enough to kiss her. She closed her eyes, just as he kissed one eyelid and then the other. Holding her breath as he caressed the sides of her face, his mouth planting feathery kisses where his fingers had been. She moaned as she opened her eyes to find him staring at her mouth. Then he kissed her. He was tender but insistent. He pushed her gently onto her back without breaking the kiss. Flames erupted in her stomach together with a yearning she didn't understand. She wanted more. Tentatively, she caressed his arms and shoulders. He groaned before breaking the kiss.

"Soon, I won't be able to stop."

She saw his question, and her answer was to move up in his arms to kiss him tenderly, but passionately.

CHAPTER 63

Nandita's giggles woke Sorcha the next morning. Realizing she was naked under the blanket, she couldn't meet her friend's eyes. She moved her foot expecting to feel her husband but he wasn't there. Shocked, she sat up so quickly she had to grab the cover to preserve what little modesty she had left.

"Where is Brian?"

"My brother is talking with Chief." Nandita's eyes sparkled. "He sent me with breakfast. So now you share a blanket." Nandita giggled again. This time, Sorcha smiled. "You will go home and make more babies."

"Nandita." Sorcha tried to sound shocked but she couldn't. She was too happy. A baby. Maybe they had already made one.

"Your husband is like our father. A good man. He has offered to provide food for me and my children. The chief says I can stay. He says he will make sure Sleeping Bear knows our divorce is final. It is recognized by our people."

Sorcha was puzzled by the sound of regret in Nandita's voice. "This doesn't make you happy? I thought you wanted to leave Sleeping Bear."

"I do, but… oh, it is nothing."

"Tell me, Nandita. We were friends, now we are sisters." Sorcha would have put an arm around her friend but being naked, it wasn't an option.

"It means I must stay with Chief Running Buffalo. When he moves the tribe to the new home, I must go with them."

"I wish you did not have to go to Montana. It isn't right to make you all live on a reservation." Sorcha thought quickly. "I could ask Brian to let you make your home with us."

Nandita shook her head hard. "No, you need time to grow together as a couple."

"He can take us to visit your new home. If we are allowed." Sorcha wasn't at all certain the soldiers would let them visit but she was going to try.

"I would like that."

The closed look on Nandita's face warned Sorcha not to probe any further. Nandita stood. "I will leave you to get dressed. My brother wants to leave shortly. He said it is time to collect your children and go home."

Sorcha stretched as her friend left the teepee. She said a quick prayer for Nandita and her family that everything would work out. She knew she should be more concerned for her, but for now, she could only think of her own family. She hugged herself with glee. Happiness flooded her. She was going home with her husband. Together they would collect their girls and be a family. A proper family.

Suddenly, she couldn't get dressed fast enough.

CHAPTER 64

"Close your eyes. Tight, no peeking." Jenny told her pa as she led him to the table. Meggie giggled as her pa put one hand out in front of him. He grunted as he walked into the bench. "Can I look now?"

"No, Pa, you'll ruin the surprise."

Jenny pushed Brian into his seat as the rest of the family watched. Sorcha had asked Frank to join them but he'd been called out to a ranch. Nandita had come alone, her children staying with her Indian family.

"How long are you going to leave me sitting here with my eyes closed?"

Sorcha exchanged a quick grin with Nandita before putting the wrapped parcel on the plate in front of Brian. She signaled to Jenny.

"You can open your eyes now, Pa."

Brian opened his eyes as his family clapped. Sorcha's spine tingled at the loving look he sent in her direction. "Open your present, Brian. Happy birthday." She said softly as she took her seat. All eyes were on Brian. He picked up the package and carefully removed the paper wrapping. She watched his face closely. She hoped she had picked the right one. Katie had assured her but she'd still been nervous. She didn't want her husband thinking she was trying to educate him.

Brian didn't say anything but simply stared at the book an expression of awe on his face. Sorcha's stomach clenched. He didn't like it. She stood up quickly, causing the dishes on the table to rattle. Everyone looked at her. "Sorry, I thought I would get the pie."

Brian put the book reverently on the table and moved toward Sorcha. He took her in his arms and kissed her soundly. "That's the best present I ever got for my birthday. Thank you."

Her eyes filled with tears.

"Ma's crying. What you do that for?" Meggie's accusatory tone made everyone laugh.

"Your ma's happy."

"That's dumb, you don't cry when you're happy. You smile like this. See?" Meggie smiled, showing the wide gaps from her missing front teeth.

"Sit down, Meggie." Sorcha said, still smiling.

"Are you sure you like it? I don't know anything about horses but maybe you know all that stuff already."

Brian picked up the book once more. *The Complete Farrier by Walter B Slone.* "It's an amazing present but there's something missing. You forgot the kiss."

"Brian Petersen. Behave yourself."

"Come here wife and obey your husband. You promised you would."

Sorcha gazed up into his eyes. "I did, didn't I?"

He leaned down and kissed her sweetly on the lips. "Yes, you did." He whispered into her ear. Wrapping his arm around her, he pulled her close to his side. He looked at the people gathered around his table. "Thank you all so much. You are the best family a man could ever ask for."

* * *

THE NEXT MORNING, Brian hummed as he entered the barn. Frank looked up with an amused expression on his face.

"You sure are happy today. I take it you had a nice birthday celebration."

Brian grinned at his friend. He was happy. He had an amazing wife and his children were thriving. With

Sorcha's help, he had put the ghosts of his past to bed. His pa may have acted badly getting his Indian squaw pregnant and then deserting her to return to his white family. But he wasn't a murderer. To some people, he was a traitor for having deserted the army, but in Brian's eyes, he was a hero. He had stood up against injustice and saved many lives in the process.

While not agreeing with his pa's relationship with the chief's sister, he was glad to have his sister Nandita in his life. She was an incredible woman, and despite the hardships she was living through, she always had a smile on her face.

"I am going to check on Sorcha and the girls. I won't be long."

"You take all the time you need. Nice to see you all so happy."

Brian clapped his friend on the back. "Your turn will come too, you'll see." He didn't wait for an answer. He was impatient to find his wife.

* * *

SORCHA WIPED the sweat from her forehead. It was hot and thirsty work, but the vegetables had to be harvested. Her first winter in Colorado was looming and she didn't want her family going hungry. Growing children needed the vital vitamins her crop would provide. Her husband's arm snaked around her waist as he drew her close planting a kiss on the top of her bonnet. "You look very attractive with mud on your face, wife."

Turning into his embrace she reached up to draw him in for a proper kiss. She didn't care the children were playing a couple of feet away. Nandita had gone to see her people earlier in the morning and as yet hadn't returned. She was going to make the most of her time alone with her family.

She leaned closer to him as he put his arm around her shoulders. "You shouldn't work so hard. Why not take a break while the sun is high? Your face is turning pink."

"That's not from the sun and well you know it, Brian Petersen."

"You mean, you are blushing. Because of this?" His kiss seared her lips, sending heat flashing though her entire body. One hand caressed the back of her neck while the other held her waist. She groaned as he deepened the kiss. After a couple of pleasurable seconds, she reluctantly pushed him away.

"Brian. The girls..."

"Hmm, they don't mind." His eyes, dark with desire, travelled over her body, causing her pulse to race.

She sent a quick look in the direction of the girls,

but they were totally consumed in their game. When Brian bent his head for another kiss, she gave in to her desires, allowing him to hold her close.

"Sorcha Petersen, you have a bad influence on me. I should be working and you are distracting me from my chores."

She chortled as he waggled his eyebrows at her, his love for her radiating out of their depths.

"Go on with you. I've work to be doing, and the vegetables aren't going to pick themselves."

He kissed her quickly. "Don't get too tired. Wouldn't want you to fall asleep too early."

"Brian Petersen, have you no shame? Go on now. Get."

Her lips tingled from his kisses as she watched him walking back toward the barn. Turning back to her work, she attacked the ground with a vengeance. The quicker she got the chores done, the sooner she would see him again. She sang as she worked. "What are you singing, Ma? It sounds good. Not sad like the songs you used to sing."

"It's an Irish gig. I'll teach you the dance to it later, if you help me for a bit."

"Come on, Meggie, let's help Ma pick these beets. If she gets done faster, she'll have time to bake a pie for dinner."

"Will you, Ma? I love your pies."

Sorcha bent to cuddle the two girls to her. “You bet I will, sunshine. Now, let's get back to work. Maybe we can finish with a splash in the creek later. Your pa might even join us.”

“I love having a ma and being part of a real family.” Meggie said, grabbing Sorcha around the legs.

“Me too,” added Jenny.

Sorcha couldn't speak, her voice trapped by the lump in her throat. “Me three!” She whispered, when she finally got her emotions under control.

EPILOGUE

Sorcha smiled. She loved her life. Brian was a caring husband, although still overprotective at times. Her closest friends were all sitting around the table in Mary's kitchen. Mrs. H had baked trays of cookies. The children had grabbed a few before running outside to play, leaving the adults to enjoy some time chatting as they worked on a new quilt.

"How is Frank today?"

"Frank? I do not know. I have not seen him." Nandita kept her eyes on the ground, making Sorcha giggle. "You are a big tease, Sorcha Petersen."

"What about Frank?" Mary's eyes gleamed. Mary had decided some time back that every couple should be as happily married as she was. She couldn't resist matchmaking to the amusement of her friends.

"Nandita and Frank are in love but both of them are too shy to admit it." Katie said, before laughing at the expression on Nandita's face.

"Sorcha told you? She promised not to."

"I didn't say a word. I didn't have to. You show everyone how you feel when you look at him. He is just the same. Everyone in Clover Springs knows you are a couple in the making. Reverend Timmons is just itching for you to name a date."

Nandita's face fell. "It is not possible. We cannot marry."

"It doesn't have to be in church. I am not sure Frank is that much of a believer anyway, no matter what Reverend Timmons chooses to think." Katie was quick to reassure Nandita.

"It is not your Reverend that causes the problems. Frank will not move with my people. He does not want to leave Clover Springs."

"That's understandable, isn't it? He has a good job. They can come and visit you." Mary said, attacking her sewing with her needle. Her skills hadn't improved much since coming to Clover Springs.

Surprised Mary had forgotten the Indians probably wouldn't be able to come and go as they pleased, Sorcha went to put her arm around Nandita. Sorcha had never seen Nandita cry, although she had been through so much already. Sleeping Bear had refused to accept his wife's petition for divorce, despite her best efforts. Brian had come close to giving the brave a taste of his own medicine but Chief Running Buffalo held him back. He kept telling them that the Wise One would deal with Sleeping Bear in his own time.

Nandita and her family came a lot to the farm. Brian surprised all of them with the depth of the feelings he developed for his sister and her children. He kept his word and supplied the Indians with food and other goods. In return, Nandita kept them stocked up with salve for Sorcha's hands, teas for illnesses as well as moccasins and other Indian items to help Sorcha adjust to the Colorado climate.

Chief Running Buffalo had been right. The soldiers had caught up with the renegade braves, killing Sleeping Bear instantly. His death had won Nandita her freedom for now, but it wasn't going to last long. Rumors persisted the last of the Indians would be forced to move to the reservation in Montana. Sorcha didn't want to think of the future when Nandita and her family would no longer be in Clover Springs.

"Can Brian not persuade the authorities to let them stay?" Katie whispered, not wanting to hurt Nandita's feelings, yet asking the obvious question.

"He has tried but they will not listen. There is no

proof Nandita is his sister. I am not sure it would make any difference if there was." Sorcha squeezed Nandita's hand slightly. No matter where her friend ended up, she would always be a part of their family.

"I am sick of bad news. Why can't the Indians just live here peacefully? Chief Running Buffalo and his tribe just want to be left alone. Not much to ask, is it?"

Silence descended on their little sewing circle. Mrs. H. came in. "The children are fine. What's wrong in here?" Mrs. H stood there, her hands on her hips. "What's with all the long faces? Did I put salt in the cookies instead of sugar?"

The ladies laughed. Mary stood to pull up a seat for Mrs. Higgins. "Sit down and have one of your cookies. You know they are delicious, as usual."

Katie looked at Sorcha. "Sorcha, are you going to tell us what was in your letter?"

"Katie Sullivan. Letters are supposed to be private." Mary turned to wink at Sorcha. "Was it from Boston? Anything exciting?"

Sorcha nodded, her stomach churning. She wasn't sure this was good news, although it would definitely count as exciting.

"The letter was from Father Molloy."

"Oh good, what's Nellie been up to? Has he heard from her?" Katie asked.

"My sister has been looking for me. Father Molloy told her I was living in Clover Springs."

"Sister? I didn't know you had any relatives." Katie said as the rest of the women stared at Sorcha.

"Neither did I until now. Mother Superior said something that last day at the orphanage, but I put it down to the ramblings of a cruel woman. But Father Molloy must believe this girl. Emer. He says he thinks she will travel here to find me."

"When?" Mary asked quietly. She didn't take her eyes from Sorcha.

"I don't know. He doesn't say. He said she came, they chatted and she left. He hasn't heard from her since."

"Well, she's hardly going to just show up, is she? Most people would write a letter first. Especially if they know their very existence may come as a shock."

"I wonder, if she's coming, will she bring Patricia?" Sorcha voiced the thought that had consumed her since she first read the letter.

"Who's Patricia? Another sister?" Katie asked as Mary stared at Sorcha, her face white with shock. Only she knew who Patricia was.

"My mother."

* * *

THANK you so much for reading Katie. I hope you want to continue reading about her and her friends in Clover Springs. Emer the next book brings back old friends and introduces new ones.

ALSO BY RACHEL WESSON

The Resistance Sisters

Darkness Falls

Light Rises

Hearts at War

When's Mummy Coming

A Mother's Promise

WWII Irish Stand Alone

Stolen from her Mother

Orphans of Hope House

Home for unloved Orphans (Orphans of Hope House 1)

Baby on the Doorstep (Orphans of Hope House 2)

Women and War

Gracie under Fire

Penny's Secret Mission

Molly's Flight

Hearts on the Rails

Orphan Train Escape

Orphan Train Trials

Orphan Train Christmas

Orphan Train Tragedy

Orphan Train Strike

Orphan Train Disaster

Trail of Hearts - Oregon Trail Series

Oregon Bound (book 1)

Oregon Dreams (book 2)

Oregon Destiny (book 3)

Oregon Discovery (book 4)

Oregon Disaster (book 5)

12 Days of Christmas - co -authored series.

The Maid - book 8

Clover Springs Mail Order Brides

Katie (Book 1)

Mary (Book 2)

Sorcha (Book 3)

Emer (Book 4)

Laura (Book 5)

Ellen (Book 6)

Thanksgiving in Clover Springs (book 7)

Christmas in Clover Springs (book8)

Erin (Book 9)

Eleanor (book 10)

Cathy (book 11)

Mrs. Grey

Clover Springs East

New York Bound (book 1)

New York Storm (book 2)

New York Hope (book 3)

ACKNOWLEDGMENTS

This book wouldn't have been possible without the help of so many people. Thanks to Erin Dameron-Hill for my fantastic covers. Erin is a gifted artist who makes my characters come to life.

The ladies from Pioneer Hearts who volunteered to proofread my book. Special thanks go to Nancy Cowan, Marlene Larsen, Cindy Nipper, Marilyn Cortellini, Sherry Masters, Janet Lessley, Robin Malek, Meisje Sanders Arcuri and Denise Cervantes who all spotted errors (mine) that had slipped through.

I'd love you to come hang out with us at my readers group on Facebook at https://www.facebook.com/groups/rachelwessonsreaders

Last, but by no means least, huge thanks and love to my husband and my three children.

Made in the USA
Las Vegas, NV
15 November 2023

80888981R00163